ELYNIA

ELYNIA

DAVID MICHAEL BELCZYK

Seattle | 2011

DARK COAST PRESS

3645 Greenwood Ave N.
Seattle, WA 98103 U.S.A.
www.darkcoastpress.com | info@darkcoastpress.com

ISBN-13: 9780984428823
Library of Congress Control Number (LCCN): 2011923300

First U.S. paperback edition 2011
Published by Dark Coast Press Co.

First Printing
10   9   8   7   6   5   4   3   2   1

Cover design by Chris Jordan and Shipwreck Design
Book design by Charlie Potter

To Mima

Elynia

ELYNIA

PROLOGUE

Now all generations live in the storm. But the storm was not always and will not be forever. It will pass with frightening quickness when the travail is over. It is the storm of jealous time and of a suffering world marked by betrayal. The downpour encloses everything, drenches the world with its plotting image. Cleanses everything. Erodes everything. The storm wants all things for itself. It wants all names. Melts all stone. Devours all tombs. Forgets all. Its arduous beauty pours unquenchable longing into the full eyes and foolish ears and wound-like mouths of endless souls that awake in its wet. The storm is the inescapable past. The storm is the future as though it were past. It is imminent, stills sight and sound, a fury of sameness and multiplicity. Raindrops whisper an unapproachable paradise, a promise slithered out of the hissing lying arcs of drops dying.

Generation after generation persists within the storm. They make of it a communion of all times and all ruins. And the storm becomes their unity, the articulation of their one suffering. So that life and light open in the gray—a final springtide, nourished by the rain. The storm creates even as it destroys.

The transfiguring rush falls back like a curtain torn in two, to the golden twilight. The low sun glows peach and rose again on stripped petals littering the ground, and wind stirs with the mist to tend its pageant train. The world crawls first, then walks, overcoming the fulcrum. Rise and walk. Come out. Draw back the horizon.

From within the storm, the generations call to one another, to the wearying monuments of lives past and lives to come, to the eclipse of time, to their lost selves. They cry to unapproachable paradise:

I am calling Elynia! out from a mouth full of raindrops. The storm teems from my lips. My courage to pronounce the deluge that renders me.

STOP ME NOW BEFORE I DEPART THIS CRADLE OF STONE . . .

At three o'clock in the afternoon, amid the blithe, floating aftermath of a school day, the child's grandmother left her small downtown home to retrieve him in her gigantic blue car. Her strong hands gripped the brick wall surrounding her front porch, cautious but excited. She passed the billowing lattices of her pink climbing roses and treaded the stairs into her small yard. The numb husks of her feet crunched on the dry cement of the walk, arches crumbling, tattered from a life of toil.

As she approached her car in the sulk of the grass, she caught a glimpse of her garden behind the house. Skin tanned and creased from long hours tending those vegetables. Sun-baked thick curls of hair hid behind the rag wrapped round her head that kept the sweat from her eyes. The car keys jingled when they brushed the side of her bright striped shorts, pastel blues and yellows, clam-diggers that reached below her knees. Her lavender cotton shirt fluttered in the breeze. She flashed her instinctive smile, but to no one. Her cheekbones were high and ruddy and it gave her culled eyes a look of endurance that purified each smile to joy. She was excited to see the little boy.

His patient frame rattled with the weight of a black backpack while a queue of teachers corralled him with the other students who were not riding busses. He formed frank half-moons over the chalked parking lot, rainbows in ignorant covenant spilling out of the copper eyes winking from his loafers. A twinkling child opening veins filled with bows of color and shackles like velvet. Behind him, the rowdy boys and the prissy girls stood by the vague beige brick of the school. He scowled, then smiled, then became distracted by the smoothness of his teeth as he watched the daily game of revolving buses crest the hill, floating in like heavy canaries and departing like clockwork. After watching the passing procession, he could then leave the grounds. The principal rang the large brass bell that signaled the last dismissal.

"Finally," he thought, as he greeted the sunny Spring afternoon.

Elynia. Again and again, I come out of the disgrace of knowledge and into the cruel heart of faith. Elynia, can I fool myself into decades displaced, asking why everything that once was so easy is now so painful? May I let go, shall I, when I know myself only as long ago—vampiric, as my raised face casts no shadow? Gawking up at the shadow of my potential. Years becoming stubble upon my face that will not yield a child.

His grandmother waved from the window of her car as it swung a great, wide arc toward the curb. He trudged up, trying to hurry with his bag filled with math, science, english, months-old tests and worksheets. The child had dreaded throwing away one scrap of his work or anything he ever read, and his shoulders hunched under the weight. His grandmother pulled a happy frown from across the seats, through the opened passenger door; he squinted inside.

"Look at you," she threatened, "better straighten up. Your shoulders are all bent under there! You'll become a slouch." She gave a motion with her arm that seemed to embrace him even as he stood outside the car, towing him into the seat. He used two hands to pull the heavy door closed. As he sealed himself within the capsule of the car he imagined being stricken with slouch and remembered the "speed freak" at the annual firemen's carnival stomping mercilessly within his scullery trailer. Redrat eyes, wild coaldust hair, spine bent under thunder peals of madness. He didn't dare go in. He didn't dare go in. He spent his money on funnel cake instead.

"I know," he said, quietly remembering the sadness of destroying the things he carried. He imagined his delicate name scrawled proudly across the bold line at the top of his worksheets, first and last, all alone in the dark, under the soil, rotting. How unfair. He would carry his schoolwork; he couldn't even leave it where someone might mistake it for trash. He had to protect his labor, what he'd worked so hard to keep, but he'd just have to stand straighter, develop a stronger back.

The car seats were double his boney frame, and their springy foam enveloped him when he slid in. The seats were once cloth but had worn to a hard sheen. As his grandmother pulled away, the boy slid side to side underneath the safety-belt, backpack lying docile on the floor beneath his dangling feet. He smiled as she drove, entertaining thoughts of time travel, the elaborate labyrinths of his classrooms and all the halls tangling throughout the school, then the pace of evolution, the effects of relativity, and the faster spinning edges of the spiral galaxy. He thought in his secret places delicately; other children always laughing behind him. He felt his grandmother glance at his profile, tickling hair stirred by the open window, but he looked away. He fit nowhere: at once helplessly young and old. But he felt forgiven in her arms.

He wished to confess: Another student charged at me today. Anger slithered his face into crooked folds, one side cocked above the other. Head tilted forward, his feet scraped the ground. He was a bull before the charge. I stood motionless in front of the garage door of the playground. He uncoiled, racing full speed and closing quickly, heaving forward with the confidence that I would just impotently take the hit. At the last moment, right on the cusp of contact, a swift shuffle brought me alongside him with nearly a matador's grace. He'd misjudged the distance between me and the door behind. It was too late. The whole door rattled in its place, pounded with one hollow peal by the collision of his head. He slid down, slowly stunned. A janitor heaved open the door and burst from the garage with his arms raised. "You kids play so, so—rough!" Then he threatened a week's detention for everyone if the door broke, but we all knew janitors can't give detentions.

But he couldn't tell her anything. He felt he was wrong to let his aggressor be hurt. Then he thought it was wrong to let himself be hurt. And then he didn't know which was worse, the nascence of the shame or the sin itself.

But he was safe within the shelter of the car. He would go home to lunch and homework, playing alone in the alleyway, inventing things. It was the time of year for his grandmother to work in the garden again. Maybe she'll have ripe tomatoes, he thought, wondering about all the great things she might make him to eat. His favorite was homemade egg salad and the exquisite, salty bite of deviled ham, finished off with non-dairy chocolate ice cream, for his milk allergy. But his grandmother brought him out of the grandeur of his imagination when she said, "We're going to stop up at the cemetery on the way home, there is something I want us to look for there."

Follow me as I run down the curve of your back. I toil, sweating under the sun. Torn like the scars of my hands from the heaving of cathedral blocks. To ashes rest, to dust resign. Flowers, lay down your petals, but only to the one who embraces you, as admiration of something superior. Otherwise—alms upon a gambler's soul, a stillborn child in a tiny grave.

Young and old, the two traveled like the seasons. The car angled down the winding road that approached the ranks of stones rolling like a stormed sea. He felt an excitement for the coarse stone of the graves and their ancient musk, like his excitement about the advent of Spring and its smells of earth and rain, salt and clay. Bright spots of sun broke the treetops then the windshield, playing on his face. He watched them race over the seats of the car, his grandmother's surging lavender shirt, all across the broad dash, but none reached his grandmother's face. She had lowered the visor to keep the sun from her eyes. But he delighted in squinting and contorting his brow in the sunny throb—curious formations upon the profile of her face. She had been both grandparents for him; he did not know his grandfather. He winked left, then right, seeing her sun and shadow, male and female—each instantaneously. He created them.

They drifted from the road and slowed, the tires smothering the pouring sound of gravel below. They whinnied to stillness and hushed out of the car with a metallic sigh. Both faced the rolling bank across the road surmounted by a wrought-iron gate. There was no fence any longer—one need not use the gate—but he followed her through its lusty maw. They approached the graveyard like the equinox: like the lie of the solstice in his cherished Spring, and stared from the little hill that separated them from the eloquently sprawled stones.

Do you know us or simply suppose us? Our blank faces have been snubbing you for centuries out of love. We show you why the sandstone is tender. Would you again like to feel life's extremities, lucid and radiating, warm and supple, as wisdom and innocence wrinkles? To these barriers, love is impervious.

"So, here's what we've got to do. Somewhere around here, there should be two small stones that have no names and the same date on both of them. We'll try and find the two of them together—they're small, you know, like for little kids."

"Okay."

She led him past the formal granite monuments and family mausoleums at the lip of the graveyard. Past the modest stones and plaques sleeping beneath willowy crabgrass, meager and askance. Generations of outcasts, the poor, lame, and ill shed their stories gagging on the silt of time. But to the boy, they carried a strange glory, they held an atmosphere of long abandoned treasure. Hidden in plain sight, he thought. A smaller copse of stones ran in tighter rows under the slender pine trees at the back of the cemetery where the stones tended to be oldest, and the grass surrounding them was spongy with decades of fallen pine needles.

The two began their search. The boy's young and vigorous body bound down each row in excited haste, his eyes spilling like Beaujolais, irises dancing over the tombs like the breath of wind in his grandmother's roses. She shuffled her toughened body slow but heartily, side to side, her deliberate vision fixed respectfully upon each worn tomb. The new tombs now the old tombs, fresh for the old. And old tombs for the young. Attracted from the flung ends of the stones' tattoo, they intersected. Smiled. Purled outward. Washing over the stones like decades of forgotten rain. Crumbled crosses leaned against vacant stones tumbling in their age. Some had entirely vanished. And the boy noticed that none of these graves had flowers. The stones were eloquent and plenty in their castes and files. But here, the names, the one thing they were made to cry out, naked and speechless. He felt embarrassed to look.

But the tulips will bloom.

He thought of other tears transparent like ghosts, like rain.

Not without rain will they bloom. Color and life make modest what we forget while we cry.

Wait. Patience prevails over agony. Their color will burst upon the exhausted world.

O, Elynia. You have been made transparent. Your smoky chaotic swirls and broad-backed marble pillars—all along helpless, all along restless. Calling the sky down to blanket your hope. And now willing to accept a blanket of grass. I ask you, conquer my anger for me, before the door slams and I disappear. Stop me now before I depart this cradle of stone.

Yes, my skin burns with the purgatory of my soul's growth. Help me, sister, as I light upon resolve and ceremony. One hand leads the other as your fingers wrap the quiet linen of my skin. The fluid break. My sunlit precipice flowing smooth like an undisturbed river. I light upon a mountain's keep, sliding beneath the river's flow, past the dilapidated house worked to death.

He tried to keep his focus as he pushed along the rows. Searching, reading, half-guessing, calling the wept names aloud to his grandmother, who could not hear him while she rounded the far end of the current row.

Please. My kiss still aches upon your forehead. Somewhere your breath is no longer labored. As I stand before you, I am still the child.

Child. Would you have thought that all my belongings would someday fit in a few cardboard boxes? You are afraid of them in the attic. You are afraid of my boxes.

They cornered each unrecognizable plot, one after the other, browbeating the names back into oblivion. She came from the west end of the row, wind at her back. He approached, plodding in from the east. Each fluttered their eyes on the last unchecked markers as they met in the middle of the row.

"See anything, kid?" she asked, looking down on him with a wink and a wry smile he often tried to imitate but never got right.

"Nope. Nothing," he whispered.

"Well, me neither. I wonder where they've got to. . . ." The boy imagined the comedy of graves creeping away in the twilight, or the dead tiptoeing with their heavy bookmarks, slinking away toward better adventures. Then he looked where he had not, *down*, where there were bodies. And he touched the ground.

"Come on," she said. "Let's go home and I'll make you a sandwich."

"What kind?"

"Fried bologna," she said, pronouncing *bologna* with a hard g to make him laugh. He peeled off a childish giggle, head thrown back and eyes closed, exaggerating what was otherwise just a happy breath. He held her hand as they traversed the tufts of grass and unkempt tributes. The knots of her knuckles were harder than cold earth. As they closed the doors of death with their twin turned backs, the stones departed as quickly as they appeared. Present, but unreal—a famished vanishing that did not pierce the consequence of the missing graves.

He reached for the car door like an itchy scab. His grandmother swung her door shut. He leapt in, frightened by the sound even though he expected it. She bucked once or twice at the accelerator, turned the key, and aimed the gigantic hood down the narrow yellow lines.

Without wanting to, without trying, the boy grew. He discovered himself a young man at last, when his grandmother had been reduced to a sadness. Alone, he followed the trajectory established by the decayed graves echoing from his youth. He had exchanged one dissatisfying search for a life of restlessness.

And he was feeling restless when his mother asked him to spend an entire Saturday visiting his great aunt, his grandmother's sister, who she said was lonely.

His aunt lived on an inoperative farm surrounded by fields overgrown with fragrant wildflowers and tall, soft, sweet-smelling grasses. He stood amidst the cradle of hills and faced the wind, savoring the invincible smell of earth and pollen, seed and season. The scent and color licked his thighs as he returned to the house.

"It's beautiful out," he said, entering the house, coming from quiet peace into her humid kitchen filled with the sound of washing plates, clinks in the sink, and water roiling on the stove. She was making *czarnina*. When she turned from the sink, he noticed how her skin creased with a mature knowledge, a feature of compassion he'd always found comforting in his grandmother.

He sat.

"What are you studying in your senior year?" she asked, while placing a piece of pumpkin pie on her worn, oak table.

"The period around the First World War. Today we talked about the Spanish Influenza. It was the deadliest epidemic in human history."

"You know, I lost a brother and a sister to the influenza."

He incredulously defied her. "Who?" His mind ran up and down the names he could remember, but half of that generation was already gone. "Were they younger than you?"

"They were older. Didn't your grandmother ever tell you?"

He paused, but could not raise the memory. "No." He followed quickly, "how could they be older than you? I thought grandma was the oldest. Then . . ." he sifted the siblings in their immigrant sobriquets, ". . . last there was you."

"Yes, she was the oldest . . . that lived; she was the third child. The others died when she was just a young girl herself. Lots of little ones died in those years. Because they were so much more vulnerable. When our brother and sister died they were buried in a part of the old cemetery with other children who succumbed to the disease. When we passed by we knew they were kids graves, just like us, because they were all little stones." He recalled the tight patchwork. Small plots for small bodies. Children's plots grinning with innocent maliciousness, unable to stop grinning.

"So they were the ones she wanted," he realized. The charity of the past—a reason long deceased for a future still hidden in wait. That was his purpose that perfect, sunny day, like hundreds he spent in her loving care, all gone. Now he possessed that day again. Now he understood.

"They were too young to even name," she said.

He realized his grandmother's search: precious

victims, older siblings now younger because the earth has an appetite. He thought of her quiet fear as illness slowly stole her memories, the lost graves' location another treasure of her raided identity. Perhaps she knew even that peaceful day the end was near.

The youth of the future locates the last partitioned youth of the past. Only the young are given to understand the washed-away sandstone of a poor immigrant's grave. We nearly died struggling to achieve this fate. We could not afford the granite that would've aged with clarity.

I scaled those walls of impenetrable stone like the mock castle of the rosy porch. To tug up over the crest and give voice to the secret I see. Oh, how I wish. Their names just remnants of letters and captivating depressions of a nearly imperceptible depth just below the surface.

It may raise them. This cannot wait much longer.

I will go to her, he thought. It is not their names, it is her pain.

"Oh, sister," his aunt pleaded, her face weighed by the strangeness of time.

That evening he found his grandmother's grave. Other stones nearby read only *Mother* and *Father* in a tough, thick language which he recognized but could not speak. When they died, the family could not pay to have their names carved because of the better stone was too rare and expensive. They were ancestors hiding even more deeply in his blood than her.

He knelt above her on a familiar tuft of grass. His forehead was on the back of his hands, the weight of mind to head, head to body, and through his skin and veins pronounced upon bones, his bones through his palms bent the weight out onto the wet grass. He watched a pregnant bead of water trickle hesitantly, negotiating a path through her etched letters, follow the long straight side of the capital, curve into the lower cases, then stream quickly down the weathered face of the stone.

The storm persists undaunted and profound. It does not cheat, but delivers what is promised.

From sovereignty, the tempest attempts nothing. The washing rains have no assertion of terrible wisdom or venerable age; no desire for the virility of youth or the dexterity of immature knowledge; no care for coveting; no regret. They are impervious to what whetted creatures believe.

The storm will pour upon a wedding and half-hidden vagrants and voyeurs. The storm is the only status, and thus all it does is just.

It is not jealous of complexity or windows of selflessness. It cannot know what one has earned, when one has been brave or wavered, what one has lost or found. It marches ever forward but is ever the same. Squinting forms consummate its erosion. They pick fights with clouds. Stare presumptively back at a source, wanting a pattern in the sulking salute.

A city discovers itself washed clean; the grass and leaves find themselves greener; flowers are overjoyed and burst open. But all below is voided toil; its only soaked, and toils again to explain the storm's truancy. Desolate figures deserted under their umbrellas before the raging storm drains isolate one gushing strain of happiness in the back of their throated memories. Their happiness is but one drop in the ravishing storm, yet their moaning glory pierces like the loudest peal of thunder. Far be it from the storm to erase them using anything but themselves.

MY HEART SHAKES ALL DAY
FOR YOUR PAROUSIA . . .

The deadened metallic clank of keys dropped on the floor above; you knocked them in your sleep. The falling keys did not wake you; their jangling rained over me. The lack of volition startles me. My keys do not wake you either. Never. Even ragged in the lock. Gilt in brass, tarnished and dark from unwashed use. Wouldn't touch my lips to them. But then your tears, on the tender bulbs of your fingertips, as you coddle my unlocking; their moisture emblazons the key and a metallic smell releases. I would kiss those tears. Filling me with emptying echoes of footsteps over my desertion. The hollow echoing pulse pulse pulse racing toward what I will become, what I have become.

The young man was tall and angular, possessing a square face and broad chin that swung down from his wild tangle of brown hair. His bones were thin and wrists looked weak, because he worked hard but ate little. No fat, only muscle and tissue. His muscles were long to match his height. He was deceptively strong. Physical work focused his strength and made it precise. He spent nine months of the year in cold labor, an inchoate whim of flannel and scarves fluttering hurriedly about the river docks. He stretched out long days as tall and as frugal as he was. He saved everything he made.

Summer was again time for school. He'd saved for another semester, enough money to live, enough for tuition, advancing a vague dream of something better. Food, rent, books, and nothing else of cost. But she who cost him nothing. She waited on his brash and foolish heart, mending his hope: the nut-brown silk of her hair draping his bruises, the intense green of her eyes when summer was absent.

He took long strides over the gravel still cold and wet with night dew. His shirt shifted loosely over his chest as he moved toward her. His eyes grew eager. The crunch of gravel mingled with the rustling breeze and the almost-silent lap of shutters opening against siding. She lived in a little two-story wood cottage above the busy street that nestled in the lap of a valley, where he took his classes. Rounding the turn of the drive he came upon the rotting white boards and green shutters, hiding in ancient ivy and ringed by lilacs. Two big oaks shaded the yard and little grass grew beneath their shed leaves. The flowering remnants of a long-abandoned garden burst in colored clutches around the house and its nearby garage. A low stone wall marked the disregarded boundary. Morning gold light filtered through the trees and sparkled, the surrounding shadows an early purple.

Originally, the house was the carriage house to a large estate that had burned, leaving this one quaint building. The land was partitioned and sold, but the new owners wanted modern mansions and had no use for the tiny home. It was moved to the remaining corner of the estate, nestled in a tiny grove at the end of the drive, among the rich giants. Its porch retained the original house number, which clashed with the surrounding addresses. A glade of pine kept private, and the long needles hushed when the good harsh wind made the house skittish, like a child.

He took this detour over the hill and down her drive on the way to class every morning. He snatched an extra key from where it dangled on the rusty square nail in the empty garage and let himself in.

Elynia, I do not forget you. I conjure up each slow breath from the swallow of my heart; my swallowed heart. Fallow passion caresses, struggles and shakes the barb caught in its mouth. Make me as pale as you are. Make me as hopelessly pale and smelling as sweet. My heart shakes all day for your parousia. My bitter loveliness; the tang of your skin hooks in my mouth. My heart shakes and shakes all day for your parousia.

The door opened gently and his footsteps crept across the squeaking wooden floor of the foyer and then the checkered linoleum in the kitchen. The gas stove flared, and he boiled water for coffee, then sat down in a chair at the kitchen table and listened. The sun came in low through the windows, aggravating his eyes, so his head lay on the back of the chair, eyes shut. The young man waited, and exhaled.

Her eyes opened; breath drew percussively. She always smelt of flowers and sweet grasses from the farm where she grew up, and when he visited in winter's darkness, the young man would nudge his cold nose into the curve of her neck and inhale a deep breath. Now, over the hiss of the stove, he heard stirring: first the creaking of the bed frame, then bare feet pushing out of twisted blankets and testing the cold floor. The dark over his eyes sealed off all but these gentle creaks descending through the ceiling. Each floated in the air, then yielded, laying down, wreathing him, and settling back to the shrine of sleep. They warmed. Her tiny footsteps belly up for him to collect, to smooth, to cherish. He did not go upstairs to see her wake. He waited, saving her waking for his dreams.

I wash up on the shores of your blanket. Little creeks and heart drops luster like murmuring stars on my ceiling. A figure above—above me kissing— you blur as my eyes lose focus. Elynia, my sweet inchoate you—surrendered to imminence. My senses too weak to contain you. You lean over me. Tilting off balance, my bare neck drops back, soft, like an execution. Losing breath, I look up.

Hear me wake in your dream. The hardwood still burns like a desert from the warmth of your knowledge. Your stepping; so hot, step lightly. I go swiftly. Dancing out avoidance. The soles of my feet are scalded, but I want you unscathed. Your floor, my ceiling, is borne upon your patience. I dance because your shoulders are solid. I am burned, but you are free.

The lonely creeks drifted down meditating sheer happiness. They were her perfect herald. Morning after morning, they exhaled with the pattern of her treading the floor up around her shoulders into a cloak, a halo, the undershirt she stole from him.

He waited, still. Waited as he had before on many mornings. Some days the proclaiming creaks were a queasy omen, with the squealing overtones of cracking ice—she was about to fall through his ceiling, crash through and drown in waiting arms. Some days the creaks were dry wood in a fire, popping with the release of energy and showering cinders brilliant enough to reduce themselves to weightless ash before they hit the ground. Glowing, serene footsteps unfastened all anxiety and fear. They blew lightly across the embers of the young man's heart; they clung to him and gave him peace. And they stayed with him long after, seven until night, in bed beside him as he dreamed.

I promise that the height of my life is the lowest step upon which you will tread. The echo of those steps, the ceiling of my hope. They chase across the ceiling towards the stairs. I trace the constellation of their path. That constellation will be born upon this ceiling, will lower itself from light steps to ears, an amalgam of love in darkness. Descend; blanket me; bring each step closer, each sound, becoming the constellation. If you let me, if you have me, I will be a nail driven deep into the husk of this building that speaks you. From this station, I will bear the weight of my ceiling where you walk. Hang your constellation from me and I will hold up the sky. But nails are weak, love, please. Please love please, do not pull along my axis: how a nail must give.

Her steps moved from her room to the hall, approached the stairs, then retreated, towards the fruit crate that he remembered was filled with books and the knotty pine desk she rehabilitated from a dumpster. He followed the steps tripping, aching along the layout of the upstairs: toward the bathroom, a squeak aside the big chair and lamp, then back to the unmade bed.

Another pause. Footsteps begin again, rushing now back through the hall, not stopping, roiling. Footsteps shook the hungry ribs of the house, resonated in the walls, beat like the thunder of a courageous and wild heart racing at the moment it chooses to be restrained. The tired floorboards cried louder, weeping revelations as she crested the staircase, closer still. Racing so she was almost tumbling down the cataract of the rickety stairs— pouring scalding round their curve to where he waits, eyes closed, hands clutched upon his trembling. She comes.

Memories strut proudly, then away, wavering. Dupe me back to the past and I wonder, how long ago was it: one, two, three years? Who has become this humbled shell transformed from a laboring man bringing you forth? Where are you now that you have emerged? Where are the days of exorbitant joy, days without sleep, rushing our steps to find out the

*world, every small visage at our fingertips? My baby
face in course hands rough from touching too much
pure flesh, they know their failures in the sepulcher
of this room. Anything to flit like footsteps. Or
else to make a canon of my wretched, regal place
in nature (a position of power that makes me feel
so ungodly confined). I am a faceless collage—a
nail driven through each descending star to fasten
my heaven in desertion. When I possess again the
strength to wish: I wish I were not alone.*

She comes.

He was halted, lungs holding their last breath.
Footsteps shuffled on the landing. Splashed quickly
over the final stair. Quietly crept toward the kitchen,
crossed the threshold, and surged inside. Footsteps
approached him in the chair, closer, as naturally as
slipping into bed next to him, burning warm under
the covers, clamoring over his supine frame. The tiny
creaks were next to him now. He ached, strained,
crying out with the floorboards. Gripping tight
like the joists, bearing up against the bare feet. He
whispered a little note to the enveloping presence:
*summer what you are, spring when falling back, now
winter again.* It was the little note written on the
hallway chalkboard that she had decided would stay
with the house.

*The moment before you did not turn around, you
were sweaty from moving heavy boxes. You stood
with light red scratches on your arms, crying. I
kissed away your salted tears as they glimmered in
lines down your cheeks. Brushed the heat from your*

eyelids with my lips. Together, we are a crucible, a twisted tree that grows skewed and bare in the crown of the mind. In the wind. I kissed away your tears, salty on my lips.

That was when she asked, "Will you give me up? Will you give me before you give yourself? Didn't you know any better than to give yourself? What have you saved from me!" He touched her effete body and she shuttered, touching his selfish ablation. "I gave my springtime flower. I let my petals be torn asunder. What could you want with me!"

Gentle breath. Exhaling the stirring in the shutters. The nights have gone from warm to cold; only the sanctuary is green with pine. White house in white banks; in bare white and shadow you love me. I protect that I am sorry. I am sorry. I am sorry. I am nothing more than a ritual ogling life, who loved you bluntly for your hungry embrace. When you were no longer hungry, my love was no longer broken. That unbroken love was not powerful, did not push me so cruelly toward helplessness.

I want to be able to give you up without ever allowing you to give yourself up, want you to take me without giving myself away.

The young man stood in the empty bedroom. The light-bulbs were loose in the sockets and gave no glow. The slanted winter sun bequeathed to the flat white walls a cast of gray. In the emptiness, he could see imperfections: hairline cracks ran through the plaster in spider-webs, scuffs from the furniture, discolorations near the tight corners and narrow doorframes where skin rubbed wiggling through the spaces. A fine film of dust dulled the gloss of the floorboards. It was immaculate; no one had stepped. None scattered. He looked back to see where the motion of his quiet feet had pierced the veil. The sound of breathing filled the room, in the white of the protecting copse, in the annulment of the sleeping valley.

Still nails protruded from the walls, where she had hung her paintings that licked the room like kaleidoscopic spectrums of flame. He remembered the sharp nails testing the plump bulb of his finger then penetrating the waiting wall. She had watched as he plunged those nails in the plaster and they sunk tenaciously to make febrile color spill from the austere white. Like their own bodiless faces in the rooms, phantoms. Vacant haven of shapes and shudders, all bright tactility stripped away before the bare, simple enclosure. The nails like metal skeletons. Each had supported a hundred times its own weight. But they betrayed their strength when they were pulled along their axis.

The young man decided to remove all the nails, before the new tenant arrives, he thought, at least before anyone else could hang something new from them. The nails stuck from the wall like splinters incensed in flesh. He anchored himself and drew the first from the swollen plaster. The pliers fixed about the neck of each nail and tested it. They strained, and the ribs gripped. Each anchored in its mold that had contracted in a fallen temperature and then cracked, leaving a small sliver of sinew exposed. But they began to give, and they slowly drew out from the wall. Each lingering hole was both fertile and futile. Staring into the open plaster, he felt the wounds. I can't believe it was here, he thought, the words declaratory in his mind, though the hesitation of mistake made his head clear. I can't believe it was here.

The mingled concert of disconcerting time banishes me to its echoes, like the rumble of a passing storm. Elynia, your time is the justice of the conqueror; a blazing discoverer unearthing prosperity with guilt; justice creeping toward the mayhem of the absolute. The patterns of pattering rain—different times and moods of her—but all of the same mysterious dark. I tiptoe pursuit, looking up for a too-obvious emancipation. She will not let you let her go. Will not circumscribe sleepless melancholy with sleeping flesh. Knowing in wanting; wanting in needing; having in giving; peace in receiving. One drop. One drop. One. Drop. She knows nothing but rooftops, treading across a wide sky. Sometimes she rains.

He dropped each nail into his pocket. He would save them as mementos, what he did with those bobby-pins that went missing every once in a while. He wandered downstairs, defeated. His deliberate steps down the precocious stairway where she used to run naked. The wood groaned. He weighed more

27

than she did, so the wood protested rather than sang. The noises were louder, the house conversed its finality, as if after all its episodes and tenants, now it would surrender to time.

The linoleum in the kitchen hushed his steps. He geminated in a ray of sunlight pouring through the window above the sink. There was no anticipation that footsteps would follow the silence. He was the only one making footsteps. He looked to the floor for his eclipse.

You shadow above me kissing. Shadowy preying figure bent over me, I feel your cold void. That black dress wears you out, my companion. You were formal enough before that dress. Now down upon the floor to show your thinness on the fragile planks through which you fell. The faceless black like my own when I am forced to look not up to you but downward; the low angle of light deposits silt upon my anonymity. You look so somber, partner, dressed in black, vision gaunt and ghostly. Undispensed shadow on wounded knees press the wood. To the break-wall of a black, edging empty figure; to the break-wall; to the end of vision.

Oriented ninety degrees from your kiss breathily within my mouth. The longitudinal O of your mouth as you blow each kiss, smacking them off four long fingers of the break-wall. There is no godlike love of landmarks. Passion the bullion. Meets and bounds: cut it, peace it, debase it. Split it; share these steps. Steps, come back. The sun was in my eyes and shadows teased the tips of my toes as I turned and walked away.

He hung the key one more time on the nail stuck in the rickety post of the garage. Its anachronism hung opposite the dried flowers that first announced his love. Hung to dry and now decayed. He could never return, not to the house. Not to his waiting rapture.

Afterward, he was left with only one lone key to the temple of birth. He was not a tenant or an owner but a squatter, a drifter. He was a salient, assetless student borrowing time with one key only, which left him little choice in what door he could open. And in that house, there were no footsteps, or at least no more the ones that he loved. Heavier, and with a longer stride, they sounded to him like a jealous, crude racket. Not the sanctuary, nor a delicacy.

Scything wood, why were you made into floorboards! Old and knotty, undulations like a breathy veil I peel, sonorous precipice growling and crumbling, lower and lowering. Will you please, please make up my restlessness? Crying out to me, flexing and sounding for someone faceless and unknown, I cannot bear the resonance. You must listen, but we must endure until we sound in you.

When the storm lashes out, everyone below fears its tumultuous weight upon their backs. Timid only as a little god may be. The storm beats over their bowed shoulders and presses down upon them, sending splashing needles through darkening fabric. They hurry for shelter, clambering for a ceiling of hope, cradling within any refuge that may define the heights of their hope.

Only a child would stay out walking slowly and soaking through to laughter. He has no ceiling— needs no mediation. The rain is warm from its height, speeding downward friction. Child smile at the hiss of crashing drops, through the blur of amalgamation: the earth wells like a crying eye.

The sudden rush of water blinds with its purity. Eyes sting beneath limp hair cascading over furrowed faces. The streaming water feels like sweat, running down necks and spines that twinge uncomfortably, finding its way into shoes that run and gasp. Labored hands mop off exasperated brows.

The storm is relentless. It gets into everything.

But the heat of precious shoulders, bear like pillars the height and changing weight above. Feeble to know and fix the sky. Steam rises from the lowly sinew that glorifies the storm by not bending beneath. Crowds, drenched to facelessness, clamor for a ceiling, but the storm knows only rooftops, and sometimes it rains.

WE CHARGE TOGETHER, WHEN YOUR BODY IS NOT THE CLOSED DOOR OF THIS WORLD . . .

A canvas rucksack crossed the traveler's worn left shoulder, as he wound down the town's mossed cobbled closes. The soles of his heavy boots were worn thin and flexed over the stony bulges, their patent leather shine damp and dirtied. The gnarled wood of the open windows sagged slightly, and the large blocks and thick beams of Medieval buildings bristled over the narrow streets and enclosed him like a trench. The traveler held an enamel thermos of hot tea. It warmed his palms like the familiar grip of his crutches' spongy handles. He was free of the crutches now and his palms missed the worn warmth. And though he moved with a reminiscent athleticism, his pants hid scars shaped like the seams of stitches flowing down his leg like rivulets. His tattered pack contained a t-shirt, toothbrush, paper, two pens, and an aluminum tin of soap. Its seams had frayed, and he walked with the knowledge that his few possessions could easily slip through the tears at any time.

He was wounded on a sunflower farm-turned-battlefield way out on the outskirts—lying in a red halo, staring up at thick green, savage yellow and sapphire, so that there was never even a war. He'd come back to see what he thought he never would: the alleged beauty of this unspoiled town. He picked up the streets that intricately laced the steep sides of a lush river valley, and the focal square of the town lay along the river like a nucleus collecting the strings of all the roads that came down the slope.

The town was cool with early sun and the breath of a moist spring dew. As the traveler set out alone from high up the slope, he smiled at the people coming out to the streets who were just at the start of their day. A plump, mustached baker arranged baskets of newly-baked bread in his window, handling the crisp but pliant pastilles gently in his large hands as he waved away persistent flies. Down the street, a tall, severe man in a posh garnet cap pushed a two-wheeled cart bursting with fragrant bouquets of fruits and produce. He edged the heavy cart up over each cobblestone, straining his back. The owner of a nearby café had his hands on his hips as he surveyed his arrangement of round tables and lingering, cross-legged guests, their cynical jaws already at work. A couple came kissing toward the traveler, the woman's high-heels negotiating the rugged street. Her white cotton dress with little blue flowers fluttered against the man's gray wool sweater as he held her close in the breeze, and the traveler enviously noticed a trickle of blood on her velvety calf where, he thought, she must have cut herself shaving. Then he saw a broken key dancing on a string tied about her neck, twisted wisps of metal showing how it was forced in a lock. The two tripped along, liberated and careless between the aged grace of the walls, in a youth stubborn with endurance.

Down the street, a quaint restaurant with wood rafters and window-boxes decked in red gardenias. An aproned chef leaned from the lentil, hungrily shouting negotiations to the man with the fruit cart. The traveler floated past a jewelry store sparkling lustily but closed until late morning. Then the silver store that sold the baker his knives. He watched, queasy and anxious, a woman deftly sharpening. Through the closed door came the rake of metal on metal; slit slit as she passed the knives. Slit slit; he quivered, his flesh opening before the ether.

Then came the butcher. Perfectly trimmed husks dangling ripe and bloody, his crooked-toothed smile between them and the café-loungers as he opened his door a crack with a white paper wrap, blooming red. . . The traveler escaped down a street of stairs, burrowing into a damp envelope of shade. His fingers trailed the metal banister, worn from a century of use. It suggested the taste of metal in his mouth. He climbed down and down throughout the layers of the town, sinking through the strata towards the river where once an empire settled in mud huts. . . .

Spring upon the cleft of hearts! Mortals made in angles of ascension and motion. Up, leering over the crest at what comes. Run. Beat on. Each step buries the last. Faction on faction; dominators sprawled across a conquered foundation. Elynia, nothing hidden in this mortal-made tomb will not be brought

*once to light. Deracinate us. Up out of the mud
hollows, where we wait to spring like the resurrected
from their graves. A little child, once. You are now
what I once was. You don't believe it.*

At last he reached the flat open plaza, where boats
docked along the river. The ornate but modest skyline
of the town stretched from the river's west bank in
a circle behind him. He savored the cornices and
cupolas, slate mansard roofs and turrets, wrought-
iron and leaded glass. But two monuments bordering
both the left and right of the town rose high above the
rest: the great spine of a gothic cathedral, thrusting
upward, venerating the ground, and the stoic stone
body of a towering warrior, facing the traveler with
a blank valor. His gaze set between the two; the two
lucid monuments casting down upon the lifeblood of
the river which sprung the town. The river demurred
under their centuries of gazing but, loving such
adoration, continued to perform.

All the stout buildings of white stone lay between
the church and the military monument checkered
with damp shadows, lights in windows shining and
dimmed, all dotted by emerald trees and cobbles.

The grandeur of the man-made monuments'
soared in the marvelous sky. Outstretched bodies
so subtle and intricate, lasting beauty that was not
boastful. The traveler remembered the church in his
far away home. He had watched his parents build it
by hand as a child. Gorgeous majesty, he thought,
rapt and ornate, so luxuriant they're hurtful.
Watching the edifices conversing in centuries, his

breath unconsciously stilled.

We drink concurrent surrender. But you want us to consume you. You only like when we are proud and fear no consequence. A concatenation that tastes as you are lovely. Smoothgoingdown. It is comfortable, being served. Why not a little addiction to such a simple desire? We could drink down all warriors and travelers and bending knees like the blood of enemies and be happy, but we dream. Make of freedom the tightness of trenches coursing time in the hewn valleys, make it what it is not, and so we cannot have our aim but its masquerade. Inconsequence sounding feckless, pitted against our mighty liberty, standing carved and powerful stone. To be captive.

Drink me down. Exalt me in the stone belly. All we want is paradise is.

When he exhaled, a little liquor blew on his breath from the past night.

The thrush of the thunderhead tolling, tolling for the crypt and the battlefield. Rucksack hopelessly torn at the seams, that I cannot carry another thing.

He wondered how many generations toiled the stones, cut, moved, and set them. An honored skill passed from father to son to son to son. Until the unmerciful speech of the temples closed the town between their gaze and people could prostrate in their elevating core. He felt shame to see their majesty, an awe that made his wounds hurt once more.

Where is the quarry, Elynia, the stone cut from the meat of my own heart; from the single stone to the heights of thought, and from that thought to ashes.

The wind freshened, making his pants flap against his scars, sending a flock of black birds scattering from the steeples. The river's taunted surface gathered into rough chop. The gust of awe and the prevailing wind stole the traveler's placidity. The constancy plucked at him. On the water, momentum added to momentum, reacting wave to wave, with each swell pricked into the full flow of the prevailing one, but the austere beauty of the placated stone stood in requiem.

Bells pealed from the church tower and the traffic through the plaza suddenly swelled. The crowd knitted in and out of itself, a single entity hurrying to morning Mass. It surged from one end of the plaza to the other. The elderly picked their way over the cobbles on the arms of handsome grandchildren and others with a strut of proud importance. The laminar march fought the rising wind, loosed hair mussed in flames, white and red and brown in diffuse light. The traveler watched these modern pilgrims move through the Medieval shell of the town, finally coiling into a narrow street, leaving the plaza up a flight of stairs. A slit of the church's enormous door was visible between the buildings, waiting at the end of the street. Shrunken bodies filed through the narrow opening of wood and iron that spoke the heaviness of the doors, disappearing into a pillar of black. Above, the arch of saints fixed their eternal gaze upon the river of life that had long outlasted their sculptors. And across town the statue of the soldier watched with vigilant greed.

The crowd swooned around one discreet sidewalk dweller hobbling and itching his nose, while, across the plaza, a band of street-weary brethren sat patiently in front of their chess sets waiting for challengers. These provocateurs did not stir at the bells or the wind with the rest of the progressing crowd. The traveler imagined his liquor from last night hanging on their ominous, collective sigh. He watched a few arrogant men stagger up and throw down meager wagers, only to be trounced by the bums in front of a sea of seething eyes. The skeletal, gapped teeth stayed smiling till the end, as the swindled ignorant traipsed away with swallowed pride.

Homeless faces stared pairs of opposed eyes across the boards, silently sharing their need for food, alcohol, and opponents. Divergent but mirrored, slouching frowns pondered over the diadem of their strategy. On the checkered squares between them, a king waited unmoved, a bishop to his left and a rook to his right. He had not yet castled. The competitors' minds abandoned the bite of the wind and the sounds of the crowd for the sake of focus: struggling to cogitate the checkmate.

For the sake of my crown, yours must fall. I will conquer or die. I am the man up from the pit of mud forever charging forward.

One king toppled slow and mute under a hesitant finger. The challenger flitted away to light a candle, stolen in light of his loss to a scruffy, stoic vagrant. He quit with a heart filled with disgust. The vagrant collected the crumpled bills, hid them quick among his layers, and watched the loser of the match disappear into the church. Then, the whole homeless cabal laughed out long unintelligible grunts before they all straightened, on cue, to coax the next challenger.

The traveler thought about going into the church, the host in his mouth like his wounded body in the sunflowers. But he did not fast that morning so wouldn't be able to receive communion. For that reason he felt there was less cause in going. The wind slackened and the bells stopped. The church door shut. He contented himself with the body of the church and its now familiar companion, the armed, stone body.

I and mine stand to sanctify the gorgeous rancor of man, the glory of his need, saline triumph like tears brackish and majestic. Fierce, loyal, broken, we two become one testament. Together the grief, the fame, the fortune; we are the human frame. We are hope coiled in the seed of a dying flower.

I and mine have been the scourge of the earth, the carry and cause of needless death. We have been sorrow and sacrifice. Parasites working at the hands of those who wield us. Parched for drink within the tight walls of humanity. Or captors feed upon us in their ever-hungry proclivity.

The traveler felt the testament of his ever-pounding heart, his almost-dead seed.

I once kept a note in my wallet, folded in a pristine triangle, a delicate simplicity by a slender and raven-haired innocence. It was for remembrance while away. Between my fingers was the raven's feather. I was the sullen-eyed caw shot from the throat, quill pricking the quick, but I failed the note. I failed its trust of innocence, and the note looked silent from my wallet every time I took money. To quiet the note I quieted myself, and it withered before my eyes. One second future roots easily in another first past: they are each other's fodder. The mock of love. The robes of pestilence, swishing.

The traveler walked back through the square, planning to vanish in the narrow maze of streets and staircases. But he made the mistake of passing close by the chess sets, looking in on the games. As he neared, sunken eyes took him instantly. Garbled taunts pursued him as their hands twisted out for contact.

"Money, sir?"

He stared at them without a word. He did not speak their language, and in his they scantly knew how to beg.

"Bet money, yes?"

"Spare change. I'm hungry son of man."

Brokenly, they pronounced their needs.

Play this game, yes, this game of ours, yes. Lose and feed us. Lose and need. Need to lose, and be honest: losing this gamble will save you.

"I have no money," he told the men deliberately. But the bums recognized only that one most important word, became frenzied, and encroached. One of them grabbed his left hand and another his right, and together they began to pull him towards their own tables. On the traveler's left was a short old man with a blind eye and spotted skin that stained him the color of the cobbles, and he had white phlegm in the corners of his mouth. His face puckered in a crescent that collapsed over his pocked, hooked nose. On the traveler's right, a tall and hollow addict was jaundiced with hairy hands. A battle scar over his forehead was the shape of a cross, and the tattooed nicknames on his neck looked a list of fallen comrades. Though the other vagrant had weight, this one had ragged muscle and a shaved head that pulsed with a wrath of demands. Both were unwashed and reeked awful. Their mouths bashed out clots of words the traveler just could not understand.

"Win," one said clearly. "Yes? Win! Win!"

And like that, he was hypostatically theirs. Tangled in the trio, caught between the wax-like oozing of their faces, light as ash, wicking them up to the petitioning flame. Carafe and carapace, they poured all around him then hardened to a shell. They rolled him back and forth between them like the king upon its side, rocking in surrender. Left, to right, the hunger pulled him in the swoon of disobedient defeat.

He saw the dirt ground into the wooden pieces and the grooves in the boards and thought how dirty their hands must be. He shot up and made a heaving blast from the superstition of their grip and began to run, his legs aching, pulling the two still gripped along with him. By shear force, he broke free, stumbling up the street. The older of the two fell hard to the ground. The traveler turned at a distance to see the old man's face turn bitter as he began to pout, his eyes merciful and betrayed.

Die with us. We charge together, when your body is not the closed door of this world. Ascend the heights of love. Flesh is your mediator as stone is ours. You are eternity through the thriving conduit. An amalgam of nothing that comes from nothing. Complexity from simplicity. Cooperation from fiat. Metairie from sphacelate. As epochs crumble, time only forgetting and burying, do not scorn the memory of our incorruptible walking. Hand in hand when you were young and had something to die for.

Nothing but a pile of stones in a field of lonesome love. Mortar washes out between stone faces. Echoes of worship within. Nothing but rumor, empty joints, shadows, and cruelty. See here, in our shadow, twisting excitements of passion, luxurious and so hurtful. Raise us in our shadow as you do the dead, raze us as you would the living.

The vagrants stood over their fallen, bending over a silver object on the ground. One picked it up and another knocked it loose. It broke open upon the cobbles and a mess of hands grappled for the pieces. The traveler breathed heavy from his sprint, rubbed his tender scars and realized, after checking his sack, that his soap tin had slipped through one of the tears in the seams. The impenetrable knot of bodies tore it away to pieces, fighting fiercely for the promise of the thin white sliver. He rushed on through the trenches, up the staircase alleys, again, ascending the town's slope.

David Michael Belczyk

Elynia, I have forgotten already the mortars, running out, blast concrete streaks and cobblestone streets of illusion, torpid intrusion, torrid and torn. I scratch at the surface, the stone, the unclean street, at the aging shelter of my skin. It's not my own but the march of the cause; I kiss away the sweat, salty on my lips, then dream confusion in a supple tenor. Wait through a new season until we advance and I cast off the illusions garnered in the night.

My unsure walk straddles the jail-bar shadows of the parapet. The river mumbles my name below. I kiss away the sweat on the skin; salty on my lips. Strike now before me, skeletons!, who ride your salute roughshod into the mud. Trampled down and drummed out in the ceremony. Come over me, tramps. Encircle the city's cacophony. Watch me inject its poison. Watch. My ribs stick out beneath my slender flesh as I lean back. Lately, I have less money and even less to eat. Yes, you may touch them. You are not alone. I kiss away the pattern of candid conquering etchings on my skin. I wear it.

A tiny flower grows between the jail-bars of a parapet. They will not ask, and I will not pretend. For all our stony assertions are wilting flowers gifting seed. My avowal falling on its own spear.

Admirers of the infant storm feel uncannily small. It is to be adored in its paradox of vulnerability, and they are jealousy. By virtue of its size the storm develops into an eminent monument, a high expression of humility and place. Its drenched figures deftly blazoned with the sweet hum of newness. It grows glib in the shadows because that newness is destroyed the moment the storm is felt. The new hum is gone the moment its heard. This is its own sweet sadness, an endless streaming of chaos chasing itself into the void. And vacates a half-beating pause.

Staring up with squinting eyes, tiny aspiring creatures toil beneath, crudely aware of time by the swiftness that the storm leaves. Some prosper by taking the torrents of the storm into their own toil. Making of the wind and rain channels for their tide of greed. Their pretty anger is pitiful; selfishness made into a monument. Mumbling brute like a river carrying the storm shed, confusing faith and might and burying truth in its own mythology. Even after the storm has raged and passed, they continue to look to it as the superior source of their chaos. Meanwhile, all along the storm's path, children dive unabashed into mud puddles.

AND COME IN COVENANT WHERE I
CANNOT GO IN FLAME . . .

At the age of eighteen, the shoe-man turned his homeland into occasional glances at a picture framed behind dirty glass, concealing the only clean spot on a wall of blackened blue paint. The picture hung opposite the cash register in his shoe store on the main street of town, where he earned by sweat his immigrant life, working with feverish zeal, blinking only occasionally. Fixing shoes was all he ever learned to do. During his life's tenure on that quaint corner, he always leaned anxiously over the counter when a customer entered. His stocky frame protested a language of labor under his rolled shirt sleeves, his ample arms spread wide and palms pressed upon the counter. Hands a mess of abrasions and calluses that collected shoe-polish, a kaleidoscope of blues, blacks, and cordovans. Oily coal hair curled around his judgmental features. Ankles crossed casually below the counter. He whistled *hello* in place of his bad English. Ready to serve. He nestled into this new world like the nail that held his old home in the frame, never to return.

He worked in his little store all the rest of his life. And over the years that figure waiting behind the counter changed. The young man who whistled and paced while vigorously buffing a pair of resoles eventually became worried, a man who scowled over the close work of stitches that required a patience he was not allowed. And every year it seemed he had to get closer and closer to see the fine work. Eventually his musculature faded, and shirts hung limp over thinning arms extended from the bulk of his shoulders that buffed for decades. Near the end of his life, the children who came in with their mothers to get their saddle shoes new laces met a bald, puffy face with a nose that grew large and a crooked mouth that never stopped struggling with the language. His threadbare shirts barely covered his bulging gut that looked like a pregnancy, with the rest of him so limp and thin. He scowled from the strain in his back when he leaned across the counter to see the precious children, eyes pleading through a mask of pain. He loved children and wished to befriend them, but it was normal now for them to be frightened of his looks. He peddled around in the same brown polyester pants and dull black wingtips day after day. He stopped fixing his own shoes. As the mill town slowly failed and shut down all around him, the customers were less and less. And who would care if a lonely old man forgot to wash his clothes?

Catch the ragged edge bending light down through the gullet. Crystalline resistance holds a brittle pairing. Cannot cut the black mystery that hungers for me. I pour out the screams of furnaces and train

*yards, cars, construction, the stained, muted sound
of hysterical life. The encroaching mystery is endless,
intricate, a curtain torn in two covering closed eyes:
sealing sight and stealing slight breaths drawn a
quarter deep into the throat. Scalding rush pours in,
pours out. Burning nervous with the infinite mystery,
without sight of its end.*

In the beginning he was happiest. Those were good
days. He opened his little store in the corner spot
and laced it's big windows with shiny gold brand-
names announcing all the types of shoes, leathers,
and polishes he offered. Inside, the pine floor had
already bore a million steps the day he owned it.
He never refinished it because his work was dirty
anyway. A fine hammered tin ceiling of delicate frills
and concentric circles looked like the icing on a cake,
a flourish too soft to be solid. He filled the store
with shoulder-high racks for the shoes to display his
finished products as they waited to be picked up—
resoles, rebuilds, new uppers, patched holes, regular
shines. He also sold shoes he discovered on the street
and at estate sales that he rehabbed. A counter ran
the length of the store to the right as a customer
entered; behind it loomed metal shoe trees like
anvils to hold shoes while he worked on them, all
manner of scrapers, hammers, picks, and other tools,
and a machine for stitching leather sat next to an
enormous shoe-stretching machine.

The shoe-man's wife was young and pretty. They
lived in two small rooms above the store. The front
overlooked the main street and a rear room glanced

over the trashcans in the alley. They slept in the room that overlooked the street; they preferred the annoyance and bustle of progress over a view of sheer waste. The hall parallel to the stairs connected every room. The floorboards were all bowed downward and worn thin and smooth. The bathroom was tiny and the galley-kitchen was too small for a table.

Each day they pumped through the chambers as though seeking an escape. She labored over meals, he read the morning paper, phoned in the supply orders, then opened the store, she flitted out to shop. The shoe-man stormed up and down the stairs from work to the apartment—forgot his hat, needed a pen, back for lunch. And each night he was proud, growing his business in a growing town. In the evening, he allowed himself to raise his feet up on their soft new couch. When he rapped his knotted knuckles against the wood of their new table after dinner, he frowned in a sort of twinkling way that held the joy of a smile, and, raising his chin, exposing his stubbled neck, he'd nod in silence.

The town leapt and stretched, growing with so many folks seeking new roots and needing new shoes to beat and mill about the streets, those who had also turned their homelands into pictures protecting clean spots on dirty walls. The town dressed in fine suits and brought the shoe-man pristine shoes to repair. He took great pride spending his days lacing up the fullness of the times.

In youth I turned my eyes up to bask in the promise I inherited by my labor. Now I look to the ground, undeserving and stooped with humility. I am secreting away my life under the peeling tin. Crippled into the shape of shoe trees. I am killing myself for this. I revel in it like the wash of applause for a performance I pity.

He and his wife relished humid summer evenings by walking the crowded streets, stopping at the food booths that wafted savory flavors of all the immigrant dishes. They were born of flavor from simplicity—a few ingredients, flour, butter, onions, prunes, made the shoe-man feel that he ate like a king. His wife cooed at the different booths, excited to try each one. He loved to buy her everything she wanted, to explain a dish before she tried it, to bring her up, he thought.

Then they took in a dance at the National Alliance, the band blowing all up and down the spectrum of a happy travail, finding its way through night to early morning. Couples whirled around their partners, the whole dance floor swirling like a carioles effect. They met friends there, some were his customers who were so friendly, and others shared the heritage of their dance and language with them. One customer was tall and middle-aged with a high forehead and glasses who went around the floor all night with his plump wife metering precise and mechanical steps, pushing and repelling each other like awkward gears. The shoe-man slapped his thigh in a good laugh. Through the striding couples and the men who stomped the floor and spun their partners right past him, he was entranced by his wife and he thought her the most beautiful of them all. She blushed from dance and drink, and a fine sweat stood out on her forehead and cheeks. Her long curly hair wrapped around her neck, draping her shoulders, and her gorgeous teeth tempted him with a frisky smile, all as the room was blurred behind the twirling bodies.

After three years they had a son. All the shoe-man's precious love, in his image, in his hands. He held up the squirming naked body to marvel its vulnerability and innocence. To believe that he was once this way, and the baby would one day be like him. Creation coursed through him. He released a river of life from the temple of his wife and bloomed creation's purity. Rather than create this new life, he felt he had created the whole world and presented it to his son's ever-living soul.

The shoe-man watched the rise and fall of the town's chest as it breathed. The chest was rising, approaching its crest as it sustained a great inhalation. Proud and full, it would thunder deep inside when it was struck. The immigrants were throwing bridges across the nearby river like unraveling balls of twine, and the river poured into their thirsty growth.

The immigrant soles were wearing through; strong, fresh leather replaced them. The shoe-man kept all the workmen's boots in prime shape. No matter the damage, he transformed them, and the boots had enough shine for the customer to see his face reflected in them. The transformation was incredible. His son was growing, acquiring for himself what strength the shoe-man shed with age.

The store was ever busier, and the strong smell of dirt, leather, and old cans of polish, the kind mixed with spit to get a top shine, lingered heavy in the air. Ironically, the shoe-man's spit found its way onto the shoes of all the wealthiest in town, and they *tipped him* for it. But his whole world changed one night, when his prized shoe stretcher betrayed him.

No one had ever seen a machine quite like the one that enjoyed its long tenure behind the shoe-man's counter. In its original condition, dating before the town's prodigious boom when the store had just opened, it was the shoe-man's pride. He gladly instilled it with an honorable prominence behind the counter, a position it would always retain. He crowded between the machine and the counter in order to operate the register. It was twice as long as he was tall, and by height it towered over him, smattering the ceiling with specks of grease. A mess of axels, cogs, and shafts ran parallel to the floor and terminated in dinner-plate gears that interlaced within the tarnished brass housings that capped its sides. The axels were painted a dull green, and the dirty steel gears were unreachable to clean. On its face, the control panel featured the speed control, the selector that chose how many sizes the shoe would be stretched, and of course the power switch. A ganglia of wires poured from the rugged control box, twisting into every hidden part of the machine. There was also a vertical bed where the shoe was placed in plates that fit the length of the sole, where it was strapped in and plied with pressure. When the machine started, it sensed the size of the shoe from the position of the plates then chose how far to stretch it. The machine was crowned with the sign, *Shoes stretched at own risk*. And in this way, the people in town never seemed to grow out of their shoes too quickly.

No one had ever *actually* seen the machine operate, but people were excited to believe it had just been running moments before they entered the store. The low, dying whir of machinery emanating from behind the counter agitated the rich smell of grease and the putrid hint of an electric fire. The shoe-man chose not to operate it around customers for their safety, but also because he knew its power could dangerously fail at any moment.

One night, the shoe-man's wife called him upstairs to her elegant farfalle dressed with fragrant olive oil and garlic and filled with expensive peppers, squash, and nuts that she'd saved for a week to buy. The shop was quiet, and he heard her footsteps scuttling around in the kitchen above while he cleaned. Once finished with the broom he put one final shoe into the machine, but when she called, he hurried up to dinner. The machine was supposed to know when to stop.

He turned the lights off on his trusted pride. He and his wife passed two hours at the table, savoring her cooking, drinking wine, and sharing kisses. Downstairs, the selector that chose how far to stretch the shoe had broken. The shoe was ripped in two and the machine kept running. It became hotter, and hotter, until it burst into flames. The store below them ablaze, they woke in bed choking on smoke, surrounded by sirens. The floor of their bedroom was burning hot, but the shoe-man made it out to his son and held him close. Firemen rallied hoses writhing with powerful water while their latter leaned against the rail of their bedroom window.

The shoe-man's wife wailed, her frightened mouth stretching to scream. For a moment she drowned out the sirens, but there was no time to lament. Her husband hopped between alternately scalded feet, yelling for her to go down the ladder. In that second, she knew she would need to get a job, if they were to survive. She wanted to save a good pair of shoes to go to work, and decided to rescue her best pair of black heels. She instinctively dashed toward the closet, tucked the shoes tightly under one arm, and descended the ladder, her night gown fluttering in the outside wind. Her husband followed close behind, clutching their boy.

Between the fire and the water used to put it out, most everything they owned was destroyed. When the fire department left the building was a charred, dead shell.

The two sat in a kitchen, friends they knew from the Alliance. His friend had come to the country a year ago to pour metal in a warehouse by the river. He sat at the head of the table in a sleeveless undershirt, his broad face in a film of sleep behind his round metal glasses. His wife had her hair in curlers and clutched a pink housecoat over her ample chest. No one knew what to say. The four faces sank beneath a harsh lightbulb raised at the center of the table. They produced a pot of strong coffee that tasted metallic from a day of perking on the stove. They were as silent with empathy as the rest of the sleeping town. As the shoe-man's son sleeping sound under blankets in the next room. They had only a few broken phrases between them, and the shoe-man hoped for words that could accurately express their sadness, if only anyone knew them.

Elynia, your shelter is havoc uprooted. It is burning with penury and its desire. If I rebuild this char it will burn again. Even the cinders will burn. They will smolder, scatter, and never reform. Creation writhing over itself for its own sake, in a blaze of expending conviction. I pour myself into this fire but cannot quench it. I pour myself into void and it's still void. A home is sacrificed for a home. I should acquit the fire to know you, Elynia. And come in covenant where I cannot go in flame.

They remained in the kitchen for hours, listening to the shoe-man's wife weep as she began to comprehend the loss they had suffered. Her husband huddled across the table and collapsed into a small space. She could not believe how small he looked. He blamed himself, his tentative absence. He blamed his trust, even his gluttony. But he did not blame the shoe-stretcher. This went on until dawn, and they watched the creeping dusk-light curl around the empty plate of the sky.

"At least I have my shoes," she gasped, her body wracked with sobs. "I couldn't see in the dark. All I have are these shoes." She held them up.

One is black, the other blue.

The river poured beneath the bridges in constant emigration. The shoe-man began the arduous task of rebuilding the store from its charred foundation. He discarded the burnt and soggy carcasses of shoes and bent their twisted racks back into shape. Shaking his head, he collected the crumbled bricks and, with an IOU to an inexperienced contractor, made the stacks wend back into the walls one slow row at a time. The shoe-man's foot-stamping friend knew how to wire the building, and he brought in another man who knew plumbing. He worked fifteen hours a day in a desperate attempt to reestablish a way to live. Never moving the enormous shoe stretcher, he raised the new walls around it.

He and his wife resumed their life in a newly identical home upstairs. She wore her mismatched shoes to her new job at a local insurance company. The miraculously undamaged picture of his home hung again on a new wall opposing the register, and again, it protected one clean spot on a field of darkening paint. He studied the machine intently, strung new wires, and stayed up nights removing and fitting its gears back together in an incandescent haze of sleeplessness. He repaired it, though he could not polish away all the black tongues of the fire. The machine stretched shoes with horrific whines and shuddering protest. And the shoe-man vowed that he would never again leave it alone while it was running. When he closed the store, he went unwaveringly to the dinner table and then directly to bed.

In short order, his store again obtained the strong stench of dirt, leather, and the pungent mix of polish and spit. He rattled about the small rooms with his wife. They danced again in the evenings. His toddling innocence grew to a brash child, unaware of how nearly he had lost his life. Then to a young man who took his escape for granted.

The town began changing, too. When the fires of his store had gone out, so had the furnaces at the major factories. There were layoffs, and some families left town. The shoe stretcher worked harder than ever because young growing men could not afford to keep buying larger shoes.

Eventually, the store again grew stale with odors, and the shoe-man carried the scent of his labors through the town. Those who had become wealthy, either by the steel or its failure, were repulsed by him. After so many years the black shoe polish would no longer wash out of his skin, and at the end each day he would hold up his blackened palms and shake his head. When customers entered the store, he still leaned over the counter, his face creased and eager, his hair, now iron-gray, depleted on his head. He gained weight. The fit between the shoe-stretcher and counter became uncomfortable. He blushed in front of customers, and as he squirmed along the enormous machine he felt like the machine increasingly demanded more of the store for itself. Meanwhile, his gold stencils all cracked and peeled off the window. His plants abandoned in the corner turned a pathetic brown. His strength waned. His son had grown. He ambled about the empty racks once filled with shoes, scuffing a film of dust on the floor as he waited each night for his wife to call him to dinner.

I have been secreting nostalgic kindling beneath my bed since before I was born. Smell the wormy must. Hide in the veil of time, woven of our delicate dust. See my tiny exodus from safety. Staircases float like ethereal smoke. I mourn my creation stolen from me, what I choose to lose. But sating love is fluid spurting in my veins.

As he had once stood upon the town's rising breath, he bared now the draft of its lamenting exhale. The air was stale with brick, soot, and metal. The town gaped and yawned. Arteries of traffic hardened. The shoe-man persevered, his prices approaching thirty years old. Old as his innocence, which was now a man. He saw the aging faces from the Alliance, foreheads a little higher, bellies a little more plump, smiling with more exasperation when they returned with the same old shoes to be resoled again and again. He was stiff over the counter, his body shorter, his own hair ashen. He buffed the shoes until arms were sore, but he could no longer raise their shine.

Watching the obituaries irreverently, "*My God*," he said to his quiet wife. "You remember, he used to . . ." and he pounded his foot on the floor without standing up from the table, whirling his free hand to simulate the motion of the dance floor.

He persevered soon after, when his wife became a sign that he hung himself at the local grocery: "Reword: for *infermasion leding to arest in Christmas Eve Murder*." The photo was her elder face surrounded by thin white hair, hovering fraily above the phone number of the local district attorney. The only reward he could afford to offer was meager, hardly enough to tempt a turncoat.

The murderer was never found. The stock boys who washed the windows at the grocery cleaned all around the shoe-man's sign but never dared move it. The square of glass it protected could not be cleaned, and revealed its dirt to one looking in from the opposite side of the glass. They heard the shoe-man saying her name to himself when he passed the sign, sagging beneath the loaf of bread slung over his shoulder.

At last he was alone all day in the silent shop. Not many shoes came through any more. The shoe-man's innocence was now a pure dream he had once emigrated to nurture. His frail heart enclosed a pure white flower sprung from the cracks of the town's

David Michael Belczyk

dirty sidewalks. Heavy feet, glistening from the shoe-
man's labor, closed on the petals. So perilously close
in the tight ranks of labor. So that even his innocence
was wrenched from him, as from his blackened
hands, black with the sheen upon the trampling
step. Rows of heavy feet hurried by, stomping out
its petals, wrenching the last of his hope from him.

Few were alive anymore who knew the story
of the shoe stretcher. And the town itself died an
immigrant's death; working itself away to nothing, a
flagrant and flaring stupor, brooking exile swirling
in its confluence. True in all things, the lonely shoe-
man followed the way of the town.

Here is the polished edge, smooth from a life
caressing. The end like a black polish. Its shine
is only so deep, and below every surface there is
another I must pierce. Breaking from life is an
endless task without its entirety laid before what is
broken. Totality before intricacy. My body aches and
I am tired. I have seen this moment before, and will
see it again—when all the world is an intricacy, and
my body aches because I'm tired. I spill myself out,
pour like a rich thick stream from a pitcher, feel my
whole body pulled along with the flow, elongated
and shaped to match the liquid stream. I feel myself
pouring out like the gift of identity—pouring like
the rain. It is because it falls. I am in the stream
now, feel my vision of myself coursing through my
formlessness, and keep falling.

In the creak of the night, sprung from its most
hollow recess—before the muffled purr of the mellow-

lit bars, clinking glass, and the brawling build-it-up tear-it-down stupor of industry bears value and virtue upon the iron smelter—a *thunderclap,* a slamming steal door, and the click of a padlock snapping the easy wind like a soft blister. Rats scuffled through the lumber yard. Hushed, foggy-windowed autos crouched along the streets outside the town's many open mouths that refuse to sleep. Trains moaned down the torso of the river, their brakes pressed to glowing heat as the cars enter the station. And the whole vehement, glorious town is overthrown by the spider-web shadows of the great river bridges.

Clouds dignify the sky's pale blue diminution. Mists lay upon the fields, at parts indistinguishable from the clouds above, and creeping white wraps the backs of slave-wager bent down, becoming the earth. They work in the heavy air that promises the storm. But turning over the dirt is not the escape of which they dream. Like gravity, the clods compromise wealthy blackness in the vacant palms of their hands. The storm is burly and strong like them. Its musculature presses on the fields and makes them shrivel to mud. Mud from their hair streams down their faces, and they clean their hands with the rain.

After the vehement craze of reconciliation, the laborers' hands are no longer vacant, but they are flesh dirty with the uncouth need for work. Even the sky has this hue: draw back the curtain of luscious

David Michael Belczyk

guile, of flesh. In the unveiled sanctuary, they grab for possession from their vulnerable pursuit and the identity of their abuse. Extending the hand that turns the field, the anonymous intellect turns the hand.

LIPS TO HAND, THE PAINTER SPIED HER SKIN'S MOSAIC . . .

"We begin." She began in him.

"Began and then," he began again.

"And then you leave me."

Entwined above the bedsheets, their bodies clutched one another as hard as the coming separation. Long braids poured from her face like rain, from her unblemished skin over his cropped sandy hair, resigned freckles dusting his bowed head. They drew their sorrow at his leaving from a fast-dug well of untasted trust, and drank from it, a bitter must of intoxication, deep red, coolly flowing, translucent over rocky glances with nowhere to spill but from each piercing kiss. Her tender body shrouded his sight with a blurred intimacy too close to focus.

"Three months," he promised. An island, an ocean. Light and shade. One burns profusely; one waits.

It was right then that he decided to paint for her—just as he was looking at the canvas of their hands and thought how they were libraries of creation. Fingers interlaced one another in swirls of flesh. Hands that told who they were, that touched in identities they had barely learned.

The painter's soul was in his unpresumptuous hands: large, rough on their palms but soft on their backs, maltreated, stained with ink and paint, cut and scarred. The pouty joints calloused. Thick nails. Veins fat and pulsing with effort. They knitted themselves tightly, fearfully into fingers and bulging ligaments cloaked beneath deeply furrowed skin. Still, the painter's hands were gentle. They held a brush like it was alive and might be crushed—weak and calling out for mercy. Entirely dependent upon his hands, which wanted not the power to give mercy. They were honest hands, as perfect praise brought forth from the mouths of little children. From within a young soul, they drew gems of fascination.

The painter's hands were unlike the voice that spoke his promise of fast return—a tawdry voice that bade her deliver herself into his hands. A wooing voice that was a weapon, a tease entrancement, powerful and misleading. At night, when the painter could not sleep, his hands secretly shook without control, stammered and stuttered in place of his succulently unfailing lips. Lips that poured out foolish caprice, like empty compliments, like the idea now to go overseas, to no one, knowing nothing, hoping at least to wash dishes for money.

But lying there, as always, she made gorgeous light despite him, marsupial for his graciously exposed optimism. Her hands lashed to his, to weather a storm against their will, hands filled with wait, warm to the touch if not moist, slender and delicate in a way that betrayed both her endurance and loyalty which together knew no frailty. Pale lavender threaded chalky fingers, stretched to their length and palpitated below the surface. So pale, the painter thought, he could brush the color from them like a drowsy burst of powder furlough. Nails were bitten below the quick, exposing sore tenderness. Skin was a mosaic of touch, clinging fast to her adroit motion, joints showing as she nervously fiddled. She was so many tiny pieces. Lips to hand, the painter spied her skin's mosaic, smoothing it again and again, tracing the spoor of fiery young blood. Tracing the fire that he would paint.

Her hands waited and coddled his impatient creating. Then, cooperating, they searched him, one then the other, examining imperfections to accept. It was her brilliant worship that gave the painter's hands beauty. His charismatic hands that gave hers brilliance.

I strip you on my canvas. Strip from you the fabric that I paint, wet with rain and tears. I burn it hot with my brush. Your skin and I collude, conscribe concentric circles, always encompass each other. Interlace with me. Our hands pulse together like an electric circuit. I remember your slender frigid hand between mine, preening upon rooftops of antiquity that spread me like a separating sea. Then fire engulfs me lonesome in my room. So reveal, unveil, remove all separation. Let me be temptation. I move in my

David Michael Belczyk

heat, from my hands to your body. You steal me.
Slowly tugging, tugging at the fabric.

Dilated with longing in his tiny flat across the sea, the painter set about his creation for her, leaping upon his effort with wild fervor. He brooded at night, while his roommates slept, his small easel upon four-foot-wide wire spool made of wooded planks that he turned on its side to make a table. He pondered the naked fabric, standing shirtless in stained linen pants. A bare low-watt bulb upon the table made a pale orange horizon of his torso and warmed the close, undressed white walls. The painter tested the taught canvas; the memory of her skin made the bleached weave seem tighter.

And then red sparked over the cold paleness, like she bled. But it was fire that came from the open skin. The fire of their entwined bodies gobbled the painter like an *auto de fé*. Each brushstroke became root in his own hollow, firming the loose clot of his conception. Each new bright stroke nourished a more full and colorful flower of seduction, cascading down where the painter inhaled the pomp of her breast in whiffs of oil. Glistening canvas like the crush of her surrendering lips; the painter, with destructive tactility, rolled its silk between his thumb and the knuckle of his forefinger. He overthrew himself, painting again over unsatisfactory beginnings. When he was too tired to continue, he unscrewed the burning bulb with his bare hands. Hands that, by exposure, were deadened to scalding in youth. And goosebumps fled over his skin in the shadow.

In time, two bodies licked up and down with the flame of his brush. Their tongues intertwined, blazing the brightness of young blood in the clot of paint. Figures of fire embraced one another's heat in the continuity of energy seeking its lack. The painter wrought something of such great intricacy that it refused to reveal itself—such soaring aspiration it could defy its gifting—flickering, alighting, suggesting nothing of name or figure, only shear emoting rasps.

Elynia, become for me a canvas, semblance of my sentiment. And I will dissemble lust with colors of passion. I gave all that I am, even as I am less than I ought. I love. I do protest I love. But it was my performance I adored more than her. And how could I think she wouldn't know.

A package tied in twine arrived at her door from an exotic address. Wrapped in brown paper, the whole lost condition tore open in the bare hooks of her fingers, born upon splendor. She was rapt as she ripped, welling up red heat within, childlike with acceptance. She did not have the painter's eloquence to express how she was moved by his countless hours, or the happiness of touch that spread like fire from the profound canvas to her skin. And a tear came like prophetic rain, a leak in a helpless levy, became the flood that swept her away, became the ocean and all the regular tides that keep so well their secrets beneath.

She drove a nail into the husk of plaster wall. Hung right-wise, the portrait orientation filled her eyes, insisting—I am to believe you are my longing specter. Flesh amalgamation desire. My amalgam, my anachronistic disaster.

So you know, so you see. My bare chest. But there is something more revealing, more mortal than my flesh. I am naked only in your flecks of paint. There, I am helpless. But here, I am vulnerable. You captured more than you knew. Captured what you may not possess, may not taste. You look to me with greater confines than your creation. You outdo yourself.

The painter and his lover became for one another a pair of cantilevers reaching out across the divide, reaching far enough to lose their balance. Each hoped to find the edge of a companion, where the two could meet like a bridge, him bearing flowers and waiting at the apex. But they only found their place along the anxious edges of quivering continents, quivering below their feet like a body that is wracked and afraid—the painter's hands short on sleep. Their extending blushed fire red, love that bloomed quickly and outpaced trust, shook like petals in the harsh winds of vacant oceans. They became the beautiful destruction of erosion. Like a greedy storm drain gorges itself upon the outpouring—she wept, differently than when she received the painting, hardly able to speak through her gasps. She felt the current, drawing, slipping beyond her control irrevocably until she was stripped raw, her nerves opened. Surrendered like a canvas that does not yet know paint.

To her, the long vivid figures, curling and swirling, looked less like fire and more like downcast rain streaming from an opened, reddened sky—the rain she watched as a child when she learned how life perpetually escapes. Lit perhaps by the orange memory of a fading sun, or unscrewing the dying light of the painter's creation. Interlaced flesh looked like raindrops caressing their demise, as they rushed into a selfless river that poured into darkness. He and she cycled like dizzying liquid. They were dizzy like circling birds, an eloquent serpent winding its prey, or wind caught in a corner, until the hope and the lust are frowning mouths, frowning together and at one another. So that she knew she would run.

Let me speak in all my weakness before Elynia only breathing. Her eyes show the passing procession of every believer. Her lavishing languish is holy. If she comes into my mystery, she is wholly my senses. Before her there were others, but after her I will not have another belief as deep. Out of the multitudes she came to me; the truth of chance. Her hands are full of immortality, obsession, reason. Her lips absently mumble my fate. I am irrelevant before her; empty after her. She is the one to look at the constellations with me, and fall like water into everything that ever was.

"I think I loved you since I met you," she said, under meek and downcast eyes.

"I think we were wrong about what we were feeling," he whispered to the memory of her soft cheek locked behind her blazing shame.

"I was wrong to lead you."

"It was me with my words."

"I think I still love you."

"I think I loved you since I met you."

They labored beneath the tremendous weight of contact. Hidden below the pall of its heavy storm, she escaped.

It was time for the painter to give up foolish and juvenile dreams of art. Despite lamenting wishes that haunted him, success had been stolen away like love for an unfair lover. His talent reduced to envy and selfish dreams, not of success but of its irresponsibility, peeking around indulgence long enough to be spotted in a game of hide and seek. The painter's old clothes were intolerably stained and full of holes, and wholly unrepresentative of his succeeding self. He collected his unwashed linen pants, yellowed tee-shirts, and other paint-stained articles that once felt the warmth of his art. Everything had to be packed off to the second-hand store, for the poor, where the painter rediscovered his ceding past.

After piling the boxes high on the store counter, he trolled the aisles for interesting trinkets, passing up and down the silent memorials of forgotten lives, wondering about all their previous owners. Had anyone once treasured the neglect he beheld: old furniture that showed the unique wear of its owners, foolish souvenirs of tourist spots now untethered from their memories, monogrammed christening blankets, hand-crocheted, but useless to infants without the same abnormal names. But then he saw— nestled between the used pots and tablecloths, and propped up against a tarnished electric candelabra— her painting. His painting. An aghast lump crept into his throat. He stumbled, washed up a castaway from a long journey, coming upon the shores of the churning colors. His heart so fragile, the painter covered its beating with his painting hand. In the lower corner of the frame: a ten cent price sticker.

So, Elynia. This scarlet is your name, your fever, your color, your majesty. Your long drawn shadows that stretch like tears like rain across a red-burning face. I was foolish to assume my singularity among a sea of outshining sparkle, all falling. A subject of nature's provision. I have nothing more to give. Provide for me scarlet; provide. My heart beating for a nation. And I see now why it was foolish to believe.

His arms reached but he couldn't touch. Tendons quivering, crawling, cracking. Fingers, static and limp, would not close with the painting. Would not caress the sensual fabric slathered with his identity. Tendons ached, and he withdrew his arm. But sight and mind scoured each brush stroke, scowling. Fury tempered the painter in place of remorse, and his hand reached out again leaping toward the canvas— but stayed reaching, fruitlessly hoping to compare with a compatible reach. Receiving none. The distilled emotion of the painting turned stoic in the crucible of flame; it would not meet the painter or his outstretched arm. He again found himself torn open, as she had done with the paper covering the canvas, as he had done with the fabric covering her body, and he did not have the strength to close the hollow space and be torn further. He stayed frozen in wait, just like the painting, until his aching tendons again reminded him of mercy.

What of your coasts, Elynia. Aren't they as supple? Maybe they do not burn. Why couldn't we have found each other washed up on your unreachable paradise? Now I'll never bridge this divide. It's too far. I'll fall. I'll drown. I cannot come to you alone.

He reached out as if to her—unsound and failing—drew breath like a blade sharpened against the pumice of his calloused giving. His arm dared out over the canyon, stretching his first vulnerable extension.

Gorgeous sensuous curves, half-revealed as behind a veil. The soft give profiled by the fabric. Your intricate beauty secrets itself, stored upon a shelf. My pulse beats your inchoate figure; my hands, only what they may touch. Let me hold you. Tugging at your fabric.

Back his arm went, tingling with the excitement of danger and sick anticipation. But then, staring at the painting from regained safety, the distance again seemed reachable. Again, he became the cantilever. Again, the fracture.

The fabric, hiding her from me. The fabric, the waning crook of my art that held the paint.

For an infinite moment, the storm splits the poised sky in two. The sky that lived in fragments of a whole, whirring and moving within its faithful expanse. Its contrast of light and shadow was the same presence struggling for a split seam of emergence. But gallant unity paled before the constructs of the storm—the power to throw wide the curtain to embarrassment. The clouds crumble shameful, like they have discovered themselves naked. They hide on either side of the division, stiffening themselves to drastic shades of convolution.

A man divided below the spectacular sky looks up where he imagines his creator, examining the terrible contrast. The whole that had never before seemed divided. He feels for a moment that the storm and sky, light and dark, and all of life exists to give voice to his own division.

What have you seen to make you so pale? . . .

"I should not have looked in the window," he said, hurrying away, breathing heavily. He stumbled over his own feet to escape and raced along the gangling length of his strides, billowing out his long dark raincoat. "But it was wide open as I walked by. How could I help but look?"

Like clouds reflecting the palette of the setting sun: an illuminated texture of relief. New whispers and bellows appear when struck in sinking light. A unique angle unveils vibrancy, calm settling a relentless flow. But I am the unseen depth and shape—peaks and valleys that do not unveil from any angle, at any sunset. Obscurity debilitates me. I remain my self hidden in a gorge of isolation. I accept the impossible odds of revealing myself in change.

Billowing up, higher, the clouds are borne on their own wake; bared themselves stretching toward dying light. One shining side puffs its impoverished chest, the other fades into a gray orchestration of sad faces. And its blue chill cycles back to catch the warmer colors.

The clocks had just fallen back an hour for daylight savings and the dark came on unexpectedly early as the tall, thin man lingered in damp twilight. He searched the unrequited face of his watch. There was time yet. He was not ready to face his wife again after stealing his glimpse through the window of that house—her and another man framed by paints and ladders draped with dropcloths, the work of remodeling. He walked briskly around his block again, preoccupied with the echoes of his shoes scoffing at the wet and gritty pavement. An occasional shout from within a nearby house marred the stillness of the all-enveloping evening.

"Evening," said a dry and proud man in a brown patterned suit who passed in the opposite direction, smearing his happy face all over the anxious dusk. He wielded a folded newspaper, while his other arm was warmly tucked in his jacket. The anxious man in the long black raincoat said nothing until the other had long passed. "What's the news?" he asked; his pace slackened like a jaw until it gaped with irrelevancy. He turned deliberately on his heels toward home, wringing his stomach dry.

His mind whirred like a pinion gear as he came through the tall grass at the back of the house, pawed away the lingering cobwebs outside the seldom-used cellar door, remembering his own fragile virginity behind such pensively soft eyelids. He slid his key snug and rough into the unfamiliar deadbolt. He turned; the bolt fell with the sound of something wasted. The door demanded violence to be opened: he checked it with his hip twice before it budged. He usually called to his wife when he entered daily through the foyer. But instead, cowering on the landing of the cellar stairs like an intruder, he entered, then locked the door behind him in silence. He set down his things on the bare wood, resonating the ribs of the house. His leaden feet began to crest the stairs, each one in its own slow time. A door at the top opened into the kitchen.

His wife stood at the sink. Sinewy and narrow, but the curves of her firm body expressed a sad strength. Her dark skin looked like burning sand but was cool and dry to the touch. Her large dark eyes intrigued themselves, wondering at all they had seen, as she studied her reflection in the night opposite the sink window. Her straight black hair wrapped over her startled mouth as she whirled toward the unexpected sound of the cellar door opening.

"You're home late," she sighed. "And what are you doing frightening me coming through the cellar door. I swear." She looked at the sulk of him in the raincoat: he had always been tall but lately had lost the hidden strength of youth in those long muscles, hardened from longer days upon the docks. The wife in her captivated itself with the box of his jaw, a lily between the slick black of his coat and his newly cut short hair, darker brown from the dampness. His suddenly cagey eyes. She sensed that something had changed: his waxen expression, perceptible to a wife's instinct, looked irresolutely molded by the bludgeon fingers of hapless circumstance. He hung in her gaze, the victim of having learned something that stole him from her. And he licked his lips, impressed by his repulsion to the flavor of knowledge—withdrawn into a vacant enclosure of a superior returning stare, with the distress of a man who has found out more about himself than he ever wanted to know. His wife wished to smooth the wrinkles around his eyes and moved to comfort him. She touched his face. Clammy from the wet fall evening. It did not have its past tight radiance. It was soft with imprecise anger.

"What's on your mind. What have you seen to make you so pale?"

He retreated from her obvious concern.

Her body is the cotton of this sweater I wear. Her soul is a shawl I parade like a crown. Her arms are mine, one in the same embrace. If I leave her, she will be broken. My mind is a ring on her finger. My heart, the ostentatious decoration of her femininity. My mouth is her mouth, one in the same taste. I am the sugar of knowledge, her destruction, the myth of protection. I am my foregoing. If I leave her, she'll be broken.

"Nothing. I'm fine."

"Oh you're not fine. Here, let's take your coat, and we can sit down."

His voice cleared, "I, I can't talk about it." The words felt like they'd chipped his teeth on the way out.

"Oh, don't be a broken shoelace." She scolded him.

"But I tie all my broken shoelaces back together."

"You do, and then you look like a hobo who needs new shoes." They both looked down at his traveled feet in wrecked leather. Since his younger days, the husband had a tenacious attraction to durability, especially in shoes, which he preserved like dear companions despite their accumulating flaws. He always kept shoes until they were worn to death, which his wife found out when they married. Found out the unusually bitter and laborious end to his soles. She troubled him to dispose of them before he decreed their absurdly long tenure. Sometimes she was successful. His pauper appearance did not embarrass him, even now, and especially when his heel was missing a nail, there was a hole in the sole, and the white honeymoon sand poured in upon his naked toes. He had been a pauper before.

"Won't you please tell me?"

"There's nothing to tell," he said, sauntering his slack height around her to remove his coat and throw it along the back of a chair. He sat at the table and stretched his lanky legs precariously into the kitchen, resting on his heels, toes cocked high into the air. Now he absorbed into his reflection resting on the one small patch of shine on his leather shoes that were otherwise cracked and wrinkled. The shoe-man had freshly shined what remained of the leather that morning. But it was temporary. Soon, he would ask the shoe-man to do a second overhaul of this pair. He followed from the meager glint of the leather up his legs. They looked sickly and thin, he thought, but no longer in spite of his strength. What happened to that swagger stretching long over the summer gravel, ready to spring powerfully. There was no electricity left in his joints, muscles, and bones. He was atrophy. His tie felt tight around his neck, and he savagely loosened it. He wanted his chest exposed to the air; he wanted again to feel power in his grip; a woman in his grip; he wanted again to labor. Sighing with pathetic unconsciousness.

"Fine," she said. "Your dinner's warm in the oven."

"Aren't you going to eat with me?"

"No. I'm not hungry."

The food seemed to serve itself in the blur of an instant, riding the creaking wave of the oven door. So many years misspent as a waitress made her delivery flawless. The plate was neatly divided with no portion touching another: the oily snow peas like bedfellows, chunky hand-mashed potatoes in garlic and cream, tender pork roast with beads of *jus* that stood out where the meat was cut. But the meal went untouched for half an hour as she bustled through other parts of the house. Sounds issued from the basement of viciously scrubbed laundry. Then she came back through the kitchen without looking at him. She dusted the living and dining rooms. Slammed the porch door going in and out to sweep. Up and down the steps. He could distinctly remember that the night before there had been less bustling.

"What, you're not even going to eat?" she cried out, bursting into the kitchen, startling him. "What's the matter with you?" She stood at the end of the table, both hands on her hips, the towel she kept at the base of the attic door to stop drafts draped over her left forearm. The towel mistook him for another

77

draft, another door, as it swung nervously at her side. "Eat something," she demanded.

When he did not answer, she glared at him as she swooped in and jerked away the untouched plate from the table's embrace, throwing it irreverently into the messy sink. The wasted food spilled helpless and innocent, having only wished to nourish. Angry, he raised his voice and stood, "*Will you please be mine.*"

"I am yours," she insisted. To her, the truth of it was bitter and cutting.

She pondered the flush of his feckless anger, already broken—the blood filling his face pulled from throughout his tired body. She pitied him. His poor heart must be beating so quickly, she thought. She pondered him like a dumb mystery that could not help itself. More gently, she added, "I'm going to bed. Maybe in the morning you'll have the sense to talk to me."

I did not look though I had come to see. To absorb the secret over which I melt sinister, in feverish throws of evening, to find you, Elynia, in the disappeared time. To feast upon my seeking, but my hounding eyes found nowhere to rest down. No decorated darling deflagration, no forgiving countenance; only the teasing play of endless lines that tease me how they touch. Build me up fidelity from your complexity interweaving. The sanctuary thread—thin as the line where you touch—binding us one in our weaknesses. Upon crashing waves of lines, and seething foam that comes, I'll be the one scantly noticed breath that ruptures—rising to its apex, to expand past its limit and disappear. I am well set upon the pantomime of my destruction. My will bends with the window light in my engorged eyes, and breaks back down like I wish my fist in the glass. Unforgivable recluse, my will. Heart secreted away, where no pleasure or pain can come. Offer yourself, spread out my banquet.

In the hall, her bare feet pounded her ascent, as she grappled with the banister. He quietly watched her sinuous form waggle away from him; listened to her footsteps upon the stairs. He remembered his footsteps, when they were sweet and gentle as he was a ripe fighter flinging boxes and storming over the docks. All that work had earned him only more work, and he had less power. And now he had unfaithful footsteps from the only woman he thought could love a defeated man. Lonesome in the kitchen, he bit his fingernails with unconscious fervor, stripping each to its quick, delicately, like peeling a scab. Having that bitter sand between his nibbling teeth, each nail ground to a dirty powder, his nerves went unquenched, he moved lustily to the fingertips. Behind the freshly stripped ends of the nails, his lips discovered a numb little crescent of soft skin. Pressing his thumb against the pad of each finger in turn, he forced the crescent to protrude over the coarse nails, and began again the gnash of his teeth. Working left to right, he bit into each ready bulb of flesh. Should he go to her. What would he say—except ask that he be destroyed again.

Everyone sins. Oh I have so many of mine. Everyone strays, ogling life almighty. Almighty. You know my meager frame and why I can't go home again. I some rough creature guzzling the spark of her life like it is mine, the tight frame tied within a waitress' apron. I want to lord that flesh, hair cascading with the neck tilted back, exposed. Her looking up at the ceiling I give her. I don't deserve my own devotion. I lusted before for footsteps, wanting greedily the motion of time even beyond identity. I lusted then for her serving body, so sexy in its apron, surpassing my love of her service. I lusted for that window, that view, pursued and desired her failure over her fidelity. I am the weak fool raunchy with lust.

He looked at the ceiling. He heard her footsteps push delicately through the creaky floorboards and descend to him in the kitchen as she moved about the bedroom preparing for sleep. The sound was not like his old footsteps. It was not gentle; it did not soothe; it pummeled him like falling stones. Where were those old steps treading now—up bright-shining mantles to cloak another in the authority of devotion. He, a single man, was a marriage of parts: each part to be the master of itself and servant of the whole. And now he was married. A part of a unity: creation in its entirety. Separation, tyranny. Should he go to her upstairs. For her wrongs and for his own, he thought. Must go upstairs. He argued himself, a colloquy of savants, each insisting on precedence. Grasping at the glamour of any genesis.

The sum shall become subject to the rogue. The rogue needs completion. If I were one part, there would be no need. There would be no absence. No divine imitation. I need each part as it must be needed. As a piece and not the whole. From the window I take a simple piece and make it king. The whole is subject to rule without power—fraudulent revolution, selfish, but too deprecating to be called self-serving. Like the frame that hangs the blade of the guillotine.

He heard her pattering turning down the covers of their marital bed while he pawed at his broken shoelaces. The bed where he kissed her feet before her lips. Where lovemaking overpowered the disappointments of their harried lives. And he knew he must go to her. In his own brokenness, helplessness, he must go.

Must go from myself. Please, do not overtake me in the greed of your rush to conquest. A part cannot live separate from the whole. Its subjugation of the whole subjugates itself. Strangling its sustenance. And in a dry mouth, the dirty taste of the street's filth waiting to be washed by the servant in the storm. The stain is not upon me or her but history itself, upon the malformed regal hiss of superiority masquerading as liberty before completeness.

Elynia, you are my only faithful lover. I will not speak but will go silent as you. I am not without you. Only, I am embarrassed for what you have seen. I am not worthy of you. Help me, savior, help me— the completion of every prophesy, my endlessness, my prophesy. I am so weak, and I have nothing beyond you. Have mercy upon me for my gluttony, my arrogance. I lost you when I demand the world for myself. My dense misunderstanding. Help me. I was exposed through her exposition, and the pane of the window became my own. And I saw myself in your pain. And I died.

He began to ascend the stairs, feeling smaller with every step. He slid down into an embryo, a delicate thirst that cannot be, ultimate delicacy of genius and misunderstood genesis. To recreate himself in forgiveness. "I am a slave to forgiveness," he thought. One cell, the concept of God. One tiny cell, the flesh of love. He labored over his fidelity, indistinguishable from his tiny cell. He was his cell. He felt the languish of hard walls, cold bars, and soft divisions, the sound of his voice echoing. A division of selves like cells, one after another, after another. From his cell he reigned, he loathed, he churned and churned. And found his wife already asleep.

He quietly undressed in the dark, hung the sheath of the long raincoat, black dampness from a light fixture like a haunting. He freed himself of his tie and stripped off his sweater, wrinkled shirt, and pants. As he opened and closed his dresser, his deceased mother's lipstick rattled a memory in the sock drawer, an oblong odalisque. A rattle like she was about to strike him. He stripped until he was naked, so that he could see he was a man, bare and real and powerful and vulnerable. And he slid carefully into the bed of a wife's confused sleep. Afraid to sleep, he tossed uneasily throughout the night. His elegant slippers waited tattered at his bedside, also alert. In the morning he stepped over them to have his bare knees on the cold wood, and the slippers immediately crumbled into exhaustion.

The hurt of his knees in the cold gloaming told him that he would say nothing. So he stood over her, shivering naked as bright morning streamed through the window. He waited. He floated amniotic in his cell; he survived in it. He tested the unforgiving enclosure from within.

Haranguing on cell bars with my empty flesh, a resonant old tin cup. Dented. Scraped against the bars, banging. My wan face; the mouth; a sip from the communion of this cell. Elynia I too will wrench free the word of God. Elynia, the half-moon coast of your closed eyes, one long draft off the cup with a rattling gasp of saliva. Come from this labor. Crumple me like a parchment exhumed and worshipped. Crumple me like a parchment exhumed and worshipped. A guillotine, wood on wood, scourge on scourge, the creaking beams of humanity's courage. Elynia, the unwanted, unanswered conversation—one sip for all our progress since the obfuscating fruit.

She stirred to see him flayed at the foot of the bed, a fray of exultant surrender, waiting, and thirsty. She looked expectantly from the pillow.

He remained, looking at her, bearing her blissful concord.

You have sprung hope from the sleepless circles below my eyes. You have unhinged my craft from its sheepish veil. Eager, like the function of anger. Tear my sanctuary in two.

And she received his candid weakness.

I am willfully how you hurt me. I too know how to beg our prison, and strike at our walls from within a tiny box. I burn up the wish of escape upon your heat. I will muffle my sobs, making a scarf of the soft heaves, to cover my mouth in the draft of your sophistication.

Part the blinds like a religious ceremony. The skin on my knees is creased from the gaps in the hardwood.

The storm is curious, banging on windows and demanding to be let in. Thunder roars out warm wind. The lock on the front door groans as it holds the old wooden frame. The storm wants to crawl underneath, come in through every seam. Put a towel down to cover the threshold and keep the cold air from flowing into the house.

Window panes rattle incessantly as the storm scurries over them, until they give to leaking. Tears trace the interior of the glass. From the quivering casement coaxes out the bleating of a lamb, a message of stunned exile wandering the violence of the storm in a matted coat. A coat sheds the storm to shimmer like the glass of the windows. Then, nothing but the prolific hush.

The storm does not need a victim in a world of victims. It only pours over every loss, every mystery. It only wants to know everything. The selfish storm attains just enough to be unsatisfied without more. The rain splashes off each preoccupation.

THERE IS NO EXPRESSION OF HOW ANCIENT WE BECOME . . .

We will never see its completion; the lineal christening and trickling bloodlines. Lamented the immigrants. We will never see your final abandonment; premitial font; scion of the grand primordium. We are the infant shivering in the font—I touch him through. I have lost the sightlines along the meat of the stone. It is not plumb. It is naked for the naked, the fecund stone. Fecund in appellation—born into labor. We will never see the rocks from the far earth gathered and seeded in this shrine. No one will breathe in our body of stone, or trouble its beholding.

The priest ascended the delicate sandstone pillows of the ambo steps. It was his first time looking out over the new congregation. He rested his hand on the cool dry walls and removed his four-cornered hat, holding it over his heart by a tassel puckered at its center. Unruly iron-grey hair crowned his rude tan face, black cassock at odds with the white stone embracing him. But his voice came sweet and simple. "You have been pouring into this steel capital with the scent of *czarnina* on a tablecloth that wrapped your few belongings, winding into your niche within a furnace of creation. Your names appear for the first time in this new world—they will engender names out of its new elements. Bodies, hard as steel, like yours, hardening from a pouring column of unapproachable light." The listeners rustled in their seats, respectfully hushed.

"You are choking on coal dust, gnawing at the bowels of the earth. You are pouring molten steel, toiling through blasts of liquid heat. And in the evenings, you dig ditches to earn extra money for holiday turkey or new shoes for your children. I watch your children in the dusk, collecting leftover coal that lies on the streets in front of houses where it was delivered. With that precious coal, and perhaps with some extra potatoes, they barter for admission to the movie theater and the swimming pool. I watch your children pick dandelions from the backyard for their mothers to make salad." A few threadbare grunts of assent echoed.

"Yet," he continued, "you will not make acquaintance with dismay. You have found one another in this gray haze of sulfur, and your love for each other is the light that dispels all darkness. You have made your homes; you've made your names." The priest paused and pulsed with fresh induction.

The father in the front pew smiled broad; the mangle of his teeth humbly added to the dignity of his hard-set gaze. His sat upright in the one suit he owned, pulled tight across his back and high at the ankles, an eight-button vest embracing his frame. The suit was black because he'd bought it for funerals.

A starched white shirt forced his posture, and a red matte tie held a perfectly symmetrical dimple at the center, tying him all together.

Like many others in the pews, his artistic soul was trapped in a body racked with labor. His fiddle—all he brought with him from home besides the clothes on his back—derived a power of compulsion from the lightest touch of his hands. The bite of its weeping was supreme benevolence. It gave him peace that turned to exuberance when he arrived home from the mill in the evenings, hot music leaping from hands cooled with beer bottles from the icebox. On holidays, his children pushed all the furniture to the walls of the living room, rolled up the carpet, and danced through the night—carried upon the father's fiddle, his brothers stamping feet, and whiskeyed breath pouring hot through a harmonica. One Easter the father and his brothers killed a fly and drank to his death, burying him in a matchbox in the dandelioned backyard. Over the grave, the father expended his most brilliant moment on the fiddle in a lathering fit of tribute.

Like the father, the audience smiled with attentive disbelief. A little more than a year ago, they arrived here with no place to worship. Strangers in a new land, captives of their own aspirations, they chanced an approach in their native tongues to potential companions. "We want to build a church."

The well-intentioned future looks back upon its architects in biological tatters. Eyes like eyes; jaws like jaws; noses like noses. I saw your pictures, those builders along the stairwell. You bloom inside the dead stone, subcutaneous in my blood. My looking returns from you to me, dead on, turning the spit that skewers dreams of sacrifice. I feel your same eyes, wishing to see them blink. Are they captured elsewhere, ashen and flat, another angle to compare them closed. Elynia, you have given me too much in this counterpoint, and I've learned nothing but the distance of dreams that they wished I need not learn. I struggle against the caustic time within me, imagining you at once proud and ashamed at its need to be.

"We will help you," was always their response. Soon the fledgling community buzzed with effort: the search for donated materials and volunteered labor, tradesmen willing to sweat, architects willing to plan, foremen ready to guide. Coarse hands became raw as work increased. After the mill, their hands received one good scrubbing for dinner, and then braced again to dig foundations, hoist bricks, and mix mortar.

They purchased a site in the middle of town, not far from what would become the shoe-man's notorious corner, and dug the hole for the foundation by hand—some volunteers working at midnight surrounded by a ring of candles under glass globes. The black maw looked like a tomb, but slowly, a structure began to rise from its grave, one stone at a time. Donkeys hauled muddy carts of stone up from the river, where it was unloaded from barges. First solemn rough-cut sandstone, then the fine blocks once the tongue of the building lipped the mud. Stonecutters began their beautifying labor as the building ascended to its high-volleying roof, vaulted above the crypt. The immigrants coursed their life into the courses of stone. Their salvation raised to the sky in stubborn selflessness. Its refuge an emancipation for nearly-stolen lives, fashioned from clay, aspheric sapphire curling like a lock of bone, sternum broken, brick upon handmade brick. Not for themselves, but for that ever-glowing, ever-taunting, ever-seducing specter of the future. And its figure was soft tissue in their living mortar.

Where is the quarry where stone is cut from the meat of my own heart. From the single stone, to the heights of thought, from thought to ashes and back to thought. I need stone strong as my heart. Sandstone washes away and cannot hold its shape, cannot hold a name, leaves the poor with nameless graves. I need stone strong like my muscles. Don't try to cheat me out of good stone.

There is not one stone upon another that will stand. All will be thrown down.

"Help us," the builders said. "We need more hands. We need more bricks. We need. The cold winter is coming and we must finish the roof."

"Help me," yelled the flailing, struggling worker, his rough face full of sweat, boils, and scars, smothered under bags of mortar that fell from a scaffold. "I'm trapped! Help!" No one alone had the strength to free him. Many hands heaved the heavy bags.

"Help," said the little child with wonder in his eyes. And the builders went to looking for his mother and offering him food, not realizing that he was offering not asking.

"I need your help," said the stone carver facing the pale mute corpus unfinished in stone. A faceless torso writhing out of the blank block. He rubbed his aching palms. "You are to crown the altar. Unveil the beauty already true but hidden within your solidness. Ravish me."

I could raise this empty shell by my one hand. Said the speaker. By my one unique intent. Said the speaker. After spending my youth starring at your ancient silent eyes, I visited the edifice made by your hands. To touch what you touched, you who look so much like me, though we are separate by lifetimes. The closed shell was reopened recently, stripped of your honor and ornament and sacrifice. I entered the smooth bare white painted over the mural-covered walls. A stainless-steel podium stood alone and cold before the audience. These bricks are at your command, shouted the speaker. We are limitless, you and I. There is no end to what we can feel, what we can dream and achieve. We are infinite. A spot of saliva arcs from his lip with the strength of the F sound. Here, where you sit, people weakened themselves with need. But now it echoes my words triumphant to you that you shall need no more. All is within you.

"I could not raise this temple alone. With all the

strength. With all the capability. With all the power." The priest continued to the congregation in the completed church. "It's not power that raises the temple. Strength is not pride, but humility. This stone is outstretched as a vulnerable person. My stone is newborn." His brows knit ferocious and deep when he spoke. It filled his appearance with pity.

To celebrate, the builders had brought the church bells onto the altar to be rung by the priest before they were hoisted into the tower. The priest stepped down from the ambo and ambled over to the bells, huge and heavy, hanging from wooden frames decorated with streaming ribbons and flowers. The largest bell was the size of a person. The priest issued a long benediction then reached underneath each of the bells and struck their hammers three times against their bulk. Bright, cycling tones resonated in the stomach of the building. The vibrations startled the congregation with their ferocious sound. The world crept quiet and fuzzy underneath the volume. All the babies began crying.

Blooming from the immense boom into the hollow of the church, a voice rang out, shrieking with mercy, one voice that was. Sparkling, flickering with a resonance deeper than the boom of the great bells. A voice in the void, in nothing, timeless. One voice crying out. It rang disembodied in the gullet, enclosed by the building's bones. It was sticky and fibrous. Lending itself to words and communication. It circulated, and took root, clotting waxy like platelets within the cold marble. It was dialectic tissue fighting its way onto the corpse, engorging the body of the building.

Speak. Speak or be gouged out. Accept this tranquil invasion. Let it rise up blazing, bringing fruition to the tongue. Pour out. Spit. Ephphatha! It rolls in the pumping body, all one voice in the climactic hollow. There is flesh in the structure. And now one voice is in the body.

The voice sank to its sanctuary, to its fortress where it resides, as the masking hum of bells dissipated. A voice like the grain in wood. Like tissue in tissue that cannot be segregated.

Brick cast coolly stoic upon cast brick—the speaker sighed frustrated—is not a redemption, only sanctification. The element promises nothing to the creation of which it is part. Strong laterals, marble columns like muscular backs bearing up, arches throwing the weight, bearing the force, the floor, down into the ancient ground—these are all mine. They bear our genius and are our self-sanctification. Around the brick foundation curled his divine-like circumlocution.

The priest ambled back to the ambo in the deaf moment after the bells. Composed, he continued. "We are from the primordial mouth. From the highlands. We are full-blooded animal courage, but with innate compassion. Our noblesse oblige casting five-fingered roots of solid muscle to dredge up the raw energy of the earth. There is no explanation of the life-root charging through the blind curtain of memory like a tendril. Infused with that first and long ago Zep Teppi: sons of man, sons of God. All the confusing, mysterious power that writhes in the soul. We were the first pronunciation wretched up out of nothingness in solitude. So profound, it culled us from nothing. It called your name, a first pronouncement. You were there. We were there. The tiny child fumbling in the single cell of architecture. We were there. There is no expression of how ancient we become. And the God-awful thunder of your hearts breaking. Every one of us chosen for ransom even before the honey of servitude opened the pores of our dead tongues."

Who distinguishes the worthy. Asked the speaker. I say all are worthy; except those who disagree, and thus deceive. If deception is what they want, why not give it them. Life is drunk, and who are you to be its clarity. You are a charnel house. A breathing defiance of your ordination to die. You are bodies: and that is your liberation! Who are you to be anything other than this billion-year exhale. Lusting, searching, the exulting amalgamate of our creation.

"And yet we were not there, in the supreme majesty of solitude. We were known, rather, in unity—known before we were fearfully and wonderfully and terribly knit in secret. Within our ever-presence was genesis and individual pronunciation. The sensitive product of eons of life struggle, at the end of a long story of ultimate survival, emoting day and night like the fever of inspiration reaching skyward." The priest shuddered, but pressed on looking worn. The new pine pews creaked under the squirming children who were excited to play afterward. Their parents shushed them with a stern glance.

"There is no God-forsaken constellation lowering from our ceilings. No consolation. Day passes eternally into night. There is no day that does not know night. And even before the dawn of eternity the sun must set over poor Gilgamesh—the first seeker in Mesopotamia—as blind lightning striking, it does not choose over whom it sets, whom it scathes as it pours scalding over round the rock of consolation. And still, innately we believe we deserve another sun. *Naturally* believing that we *deserve* eternity! There is no creature, no living thing in this world that does not die. And yet from the earliest moment, we seek more; against everything we have seen, we believe we deserve something unique among creation. Look to Egypt preparing bodies for the afterlife. How they treasured the body, cared for it, preserved it—all their embalming machinations—so that it might walk again. But it was not the body: they were crying out to be saved. They knew innately—there is no consolation that my own flesh can provide. We are canopic jars. Our flesh must be patient and it will receive consolation.

"The day slips eternally into blackness, like the unexpected sound of our own voice scaring us. Add another R. Scarring us, a blemish to cover the void of knowledge, the fear of what will catch us when we pour out and gasp in awe that the sleeping sun is getting sleepier. It is geminating in your direction. We live today in the sepulcher of these ideas. They process emancipated from the opaque history of our progression. And like thought itself, our lowliness is made awesome." The priest looked out at the black Os of quietly gaping mouths.

Let me soothe the struggling body, the complexity alighting on your ancient and unapproachable face. Let me soothe the perplexity of your complicity. You are my admiration and desire. I am shaking with the ecstasy of your parousia. Reluctantly, I kiss the dirty mouth with the golden tongue and venerate the word. Very reluctantly first I kiss. For one brief second it is an act of veneration. But more and more thoughts untether. In the kiss, I supplicate my hunger. Thoughts double. Listen, I'll only be trouble for you. Go inside, I don't want to get you in trouble. I depart the fidelity of your veneration like a poor girl in the mists outside her cellar door, with the wet of her kiss still upon my lips.

And the next day I found the speaker inhaling deep at his podium, preparing, as I entered.

Uncertain applause heartened the priest. He stepped down and the crowd rose to its feet, looking at each other, enlivened. Some stretched toward the ceiling. They descended the tall stairs unraveling from the mouth of the church, graciously, cautiously: the couples arm in arm, the elderly clutching offspring for balance. The father, feeling all they achieved was very good. That evening, the last of the builders used block and tackle and a woven rope to hoist the bells and position them atop the towers. Curious children examined the rope and found it was thicker than their arms.

The builders constructed their church at the peak of their strength and afterward they began to diminish. Their bodies were broken and tired. They had worked too hard for too long. They went to the church, their achievement, to salve their wounds with words, and they aged. Under hunger that the nimble tongue longs upon, under the tissue, under the sight of the church they raised: the body of the builders could not repose forever. Their brightness of devotion to build, like fire, could not help but consume. Years passed. The builders were content to see their youngest marry on the altar they had raised, to host their families at Sunday breakfast, and on Friday nights to drink and dance to the fiddle racing in arthritic hands.

Meanwhile, the furnaces appetite for fire grew, a testifying filament in the night sky. And the immigrants yearned with it in their decomposition, watching their daughters ride sleds in long dresses and the boys throw shovelfuls of sooty snow at each other. Suitors visited their houses in twill jackets and big cigars, on Sundays, when they had off from the mill and were clean. And the builders, old before their time, took to drinking away their meager pensions at corner bars with forgetful friends.

David Michael Belczyk

At last, "Your father is gone," said a mother to her eldest daughter, who remembered him in a fine black suit with his little girl at the front of the congregation in the new church. "We all need bread more than you need school. It will only be harder if you fuss." And the father lay on ice only three blocks away, coins over his eyes in the same tattered suit which fit loosely over his thinned muscles. He faced the ceiling, reposed in the wash of footsteps waking him above. The daughter cried because she loved school, wept day after day, alone in the cavernous empty body of the church. She spent her fatherless evenings hurrying through narrow openings between bar stools, hoisting overhead an unbalanced tray filled with beer steins. The smell of butter and onions, whiskey and stout, sweat, and oppressive smoke thick in her delicate nose. She cradled the tray and lowered it from her shoulder to the counter with remarkable strength that betrayed her petite appearance. Her tips lay crumpled upon the tray. She hated the harsh, overworked eyes of the men staring and beaming bleached when she walked from their tables. But she shook forgiveness from her curled locks and counted. One, two for the food, one for Christmas, three for rent. Her fatherless love, unschooled eyes, chose the coarse, servile love of a staring man on his way to war: who was never the same when he returned, but was a good-hearted man who cared for the family and allowed her the charity of bringing unfortunates into the home when they lost their lives to fire.

One by one, the builders went the way of the father. And eventually the mills went the way of the builders. After a life of sacrifice, they hoped the next generation could fit its boot into their niche.

Do not relinquish the first taste of the nectar that moves in history's veins; nectar made sweet by squalid paucity, coalescing the pumping paroxysms that spilt open history's inner machinations.

Even after a life of sacrifice, they had not made enough money to have their names upon their gravestones. Their children could not pay a stonecutter, and the friends who cut the stones for the church were already long dead. All of them gone ahead to test the backbone of their creation. The cemetery was filled with final incantations poorly marked, only "mother" or "father," written in a foreign script.

We immortal artists. We mortals who make immortal art. We artists of immortality. Lush sapped with its sweet nectar. We squander talent and time. It is not our end we should fear but the recurring end of our world—moths circling the stubble, dancing in the dry undergrowth. The dance dies with the moth. And our creation ends before we do. Our admiration, our sunsets, are unsown thread—the spark in the stubble, the fire of our long view. Do we know yet what we give as creators; without the medium of our creation, only a dance.

Grandchildren, even great-grandchildren, came into the body, into the church, shivering and wailing naked under the baptismal water, one voice crying out in the hollow. Their pure reverence echoed from the stone laid in place like catacombs, their squirming bodies entombed in the stone of the font. But though the children came, there were not enough. The waters of the font poured out and became barren. The keening in the chest of the church became a whisper and was so quiet that it was snuffed like a candle. The church was a victim of time and debt and pride. The legacy of the builders, the work of their hands, followed its creators back into the grave of its foundation and came to its end: swollen, a hematoma, with its last bludgeoned incantation a hollow brick shell, rotten and invaded through its missing windows by the rain and the wind. The autumn leaves rustled, dancing in the sunlit sanctuary, celebrating like an heir at the inheritance. The church was the victim of the tissue upon its frame, lapping so always against itself that it erodes in devotion. Its towering steeples looked out majestically, but the aorta of its doors would not receive. Hired laborers stripped the bells from the towers, and they were sold as scrap.

Will you ever tower over the torch of mind— throats twisting muscular and grotesque to cull. Tower over the displacement that mourns in the law of debt, in the straight lines of its descent upon us like a windless rain. Mourning expiation.

Stripped the jewels from the crown: a skirt over an empty table. Lifting it out of immature curiosity, as if one might know the world if only to see under that skirt. It swayed with the wind coming through the shattered doors and lifted, revealing only slightly;

shrill curiosity filling and brimming.

There was nothing fresh, young, or beautiful beneath the table skirt. There was nothing but the trickster wind. The lifeless building did not pulse. An emaciated boney cage. Its structure—the elements of its strength—once its lever, its fulcrum, its ribs, now enclosed in living slats dying. Its tissue fled tactility towards the lavishly private—personal gnosis not in a person but in personification. The line was plumb from the broken immigrant smile to the broken brick; the ashen, stoic face of the father-builder raised itself skyward; the swollen hands to lift a casket, tenderly trembling. The building closed. Sparking memories of its faces looked upon those vandals who vocalized in its bones.

The speaker engorged in emptiness. This tough sinew, he shouted and beat his chest. The thud resonated in the bones. See this power. What could you need. See what we raise with our brawn, with our mind. We are the soul of the world. And this muscle can make muscle—tear it and it will grow larger. Claim yourself. Know your power, the extent of your majesty. You need nothing that is not already within you. Even our ancients knew how to master our humanity: the Egyptians developed numerous methods of contraception.

Lonely jobless shadows passed the building kicking dejected stones with their tattered shoes. The blank edifice shone in the ghastly lights like self-sufficiency. These descendants were not like the builders. They wore pampered exteriors but

David Michael Belczyk

had rough insides; their ancestors had uncomely
bodies that protected beauty. The tough descendants
found the bricks of the old church cold and hard
and equally invulnerable. They said, "I hope this
newly arrived speaker will make something of this
cruel husk. Something I can digest." They watched
impatient, coming no closer than across the street,
an exquisite pronunciation in silent vigil, like eroded
words. They watched and waited with a sad realism
that springs from dispatched romance. They chiseled
as scriveners on the body. Eyes like eyes, jaws like
jaws, defacing the builders in the guise of questions.

*Elynia, be my genovillere, and make me kneel. You
are my one admiration, my one desire. I am shaking
with the ecstasy of your parousia. You are the
dominion of the knot within the wood of my table—
interstitial and inseparable—the noble hope of a new
branch. I was afraid when I found the empty church,
afraid the word departed the body and the body died
of separation. But now I know the word is the body.
Let me speak you, Elynia, in all my weakness before
your only breathing. And fall with me like water
into everything that ever was. Let me approach with
reverence the vague stone. The last stone where I can
rest my reverence; the grave; the stone cut from the
meat of my own heart. Spring after spring, the candle
by your stone was filled with bees when I came to
visit you, and I was stung.*

A new voice, precise and quick, rose in the second dawn of the same hollowness. The speaker stood at a stainless-steel podium, isolated in the half-moon nave where the altar once stood. The stained glass replaced with clear; the walls washed bone white; the doors repaired. The speakers handsome hair was thick like a potato sack and deliberately parted. The beautiful softness of his face shone bright in the light, no mar, no hint of suffering. Manicured hands gripped the steel, bulging masculine knuckles and veins. But the speaker's voice had no soft flesh to caress with its elocution, just the salvage of a remaining skeleton. It raked hard against the ears, rejected by the unliving surfaces. It rose not from tissue or even the wild smile of tissue's rancor, but from inside the guts, from things devoured. Something rumbles around in the intestines—comes up hot and acidic—pouring out.

"I am the individual," the speaker declared. "I am fully capable. You have the body. I have the words of liberation."

You may pierce me. I am the deepest well of intent. I am the bedrock. The perforations in culpability. I am the crucible to burn the twisted trees that grow askew in the mind. I am the shape and the shape of things to come. I am tough to chew, and you'll wish to spit me out. I am stringy; I am tendrils; I am lean meat. I am never a sign but a very lustrous signal. I creep like buzzard's breath towards hips, as

103

emaciated as I choose. Grubbing for you. Rooting through your remnants.

Listeners sat like corpses in the ancient pews. With truculent communication well-grooved, the speaker delivered answers to questions unasked. All victims of rote exchange of meaningless sound. Victimized into automatic autonomy by rote exercise of sound. The building choked; though it teemed with words, nothing thrived. The thick words stopped its breath. The flow of language poured scattered upon the building, the silent and emaciated victim of accretion. The mouths that spit the words waited hungry for the avulsion. Sediment to bury the building with mounding volume, to silence its divulging pulse. Tonguing against the syllables, the words spit rough like gravel—the spittle in the mortar in the joints, all joints bending to bow, to the mud or to the saliva that mixes. But both are the joint that bends, supple to task but able to stand firm.

"We've had an emergency. It's the speaker, he's choked."

"How."

"He was so eloquent, his annunciation so complete and so discernable, that he choked on the pronunciation of a word."

"What word."

"Constitution."

"Constitution."

"Yes, he was discussing the importance of having a strong constitution: describing the nature of the individual with such fervor that the word hung in his throat. He had marshaled the C supplely, gently cresting over its rockier moments. He emptied himself to resonate open with the hollow sound of the O, and then he fulfilled it with the resolution of the strong N. His S was stately and gracious, and he ascended even higher when he crowned it with the crisp brilliance of the T. But it was the swallowed U, and the IT that paves the way to the U's demise, that he could not muster. He sputtered, trying to get it out, but he had locked on the perfect pronunciation and would not release."

The storm finds being alone uncouth and bereaves its forfeit of brightness to its shadowy lonesome. For succor, keening about its creature, is the unseen symbiotic wind, playing with the world with pitying caprice. To the sky the wind is a transient tenant. A room letter. A mercenary. But to the small world below, the wind is a sweeping wish, a lifting whisper, the shaking flesh of sleep. It moves; it toys. In the ripe liberty between earth and sky, the wind holds sway. Bullying the storm that assents. Choosing what the rain shall lament. The storm, without its companion, has the strength only to weep and weep, professing an upright heart in sheer lines.

Likewise, the wind fears being alone, thinks it deserves the storm. It wants power over something it can move. It will tremble in resonance, will agitate anything for company. Trash hurls aimlessly along the pitch of the alleys. Fences bang and wail metallically. Newspapers spill open their chattering insides, scuttling imperfections on the concrete. Trees shutter, their broad limbs sound a hoary moan, nimble branches whistle and whip wild desperation, trying to hew shelter from the air. The wind is careless with its affection.

And the dust. Before the rain comes, the wind lifts arid dirt, lone gravel, and grit like waves of hail to pelt the solemn buildings and emptying streets. A rough, suffocating specter rolls on the land and treats all alike as withering kindling sapped and impatiently cracking, aching to be deathly dry as the dust. A moment before the storm, a riotous and curvaceous wind roars down the streets in a blast. The supine dust rises to meet the flinching eyes. It travels with the wind, demanding admission to paradise. Shut the door. Shut the window. The dirt pours in on that gust. We'll be cleaning all afternoon.

A MAN HURRIES PAST, HIS HEART PUMPING OUT THE CLANGING SHACKLES OF HIS BONES . . .

A man hurries past, his heart pumping out the clanging shackles of his bones. Drip. Drip. Down. Down. Fear is etched upon his ashen face. The invasion comes, and he has nowhere to hide. He plunges deeper and deeper into the dark and cavernous ramparts, waving a torch over stone that has not seen daylight in centuries. Stifling must is mixed with smoke, and O the clanging voices slide down the stairs behind him. His aching, heaving chest hurrying out the depleted breath; his terrific heart thrashing its horns and looking to gore something. I govern the negotiations of his feet—so gentle the footfalls, soft and quick. He is a dimple of condensation erect upon my cold face, as his once-frantic face is slathered in sweat. He can taste in the corners of his mouth, sticky and courting the dirt that will bury his escape. His toes spring against the solid rock of the steps: lower into the belly of stone.

Afterwards, his feet buck wild against the rampart walls, the grim execution of justice. He is the summary of the conqueror—the discoverer who unearths and metes prosperity and guilt. Justice creeping toward the mayhem of the absolute. I emulate the circle of the diadem. The stony circle tourniquet—graft me

onto our unending struggle—so I may feel myself
raking through millennia of graves.

It was early May when the traveler's curiosity
pushed through the sieve of the canals on a sailboat
with a broken mast. Long days of focus at the wheel
of the boat and hard work operating locks sent him
to bed early with stiff hands, feeling he had wound
further into a labyrinth with no easy escape.

He woke in the predawn, facing the demilune
through a small side porthole. The traveler's waning
face silver under the moon spoke endurance but
nothing of temperance. Gaunt eyes rolled side to
side, restless with the knowledge that more sleep
would not come. He rolled from his berth, an
aluminum frame stretched with canvas that folded
against the wall of the cabin with a series of pulleys.
The cramped space below deck pressed in on him
as he nimbly darted about the dark for his coat and
boots, hunching his back where he could not stand.
He stowed the berth and fired the propane stove for
coffee, lurching across the galley with the slovenly
grace of a sailor: he balanced within the sluggish
hulk shifting asleep upon the water, muscles locked
in position while surroundings tumbled, strong
only where necessary and otherwise a body lulling
limp that is unimpressed with any wasted effort. A
heavy backpack that had dominated his youth gave
him a folded posture that felt comfortable as he
crouched about, rattling through the enamel cups
and fruit hung in netted twine from the cabin-top.
Now he carried very little. Dressed, and warm, he

went above. The sun was hitting the horizon as the engine primed, the prop greased, the lines cast off, and another day of solitude approached.

His boat was a twenty-nine foot sloop, determined enough to cruise and light enough to race. But a year earlier, he had her close-hulled with all sheets winched in tight, speeding towards a large harbor with a bridge over the mouth. He had not accounted for the height of the tide. Lying along the length of the boat, protruding at either end, the remainder of the mast was lifted on two makeshift wooden braces bolted to the hull in an X. His heart sank while drilling the holes. Damage was the only way to transport damage. The stump of the remaining mast still rose from the center of the boat wearing its splintered crown. Without the money for repairs, the traveler decided to motor north along the canals, bisecting the country instead of sailing through the straits and around the coast.

Days on the canals thrashed awkwardly between extremes of frosty nights and blistering sunny afternoons. During the noon heat, the traveler worked shirtless on deck, as the sun progressively darkened his skin. White to pink, pink to red, red to brown, again seeking the sting of red luster. Over two weeks his color developed incrementally, inching closer to the brown canal water below him. Nights, in contrast, dressed him with their icy hands. His red skin took time to cure as his heavy jacket sealed out the cold Spring, the cold growth forcing itself. He kept below to escape the wind. As each day ended, the traveler had to remind himself what day it was, because the formula of every day was so similar. Even the beauty of the rolling hills and farms, sunflower fields and lowing cattle, made him suspicious he had seen it somewhere before.

One evening, the chill set again upon the heels of the lowering sun as the boat muttered along the glassy surface of a river that threaded itself effortlessly through the interlaced canals. He entered a town, through the needle-eyes of stone arch bridges that connected an historic district on the west bank of the river to a new growing annex in the east. The town's windows glowed faint at dusk. A dock ran the length of an open plaza along the west bank. Medieval squat stone buildings with decorative roofs and carvings surrounded the plaza and ran up a hillside toward its peak. The traveler eased the boat gently to its berth and leapt from the bow with lines, tying off for the night.

Over and over, twist under and pull. Once around the base so it won't slack. Shank the frayed line. No, it is unnecessary, could appear pompous. But tie the knot tight so it will get a good hold. So it will squeeze out life.

Chapped hands resisted splinters and cuts by the shards of the rough rope.

Climbing aboard once again, he silenced the engine with a flick of the key in the companionway and the boat slept alongside other dark bodies lying in the half-empty dock. He was satisfied. It was an easy single-handed dock, with barren slips fore and aft.

And if no one docked throughout the night, it would be an easy out early in the morning.

He stood on the deck and saw the quieted town quitting the day. The town was vulgar to him. Overstated, loud, obnoxious, and spoilt. He took only a momentary interest in the flowery stone of the large monument and steeples that sat, he thought, like proud bookends on either side of the town, with their carved edifices leaping out to imitate life. There was nothing comely about faces presuming beauty. Something self-gratifying about their imitations. He did not fuss like the stone and was not vogue. Volant stones. Covered, too, with soot, like the faces of children at play in the mud.

And after scared nobles hid in the descending shadows; after all the conquered old went down into the earth; this is what soldiers saw climbing up from the ditch clotted with mud. When they finally washed their faces clean: one mottled face longing at the other. Where bodies were torn at the seams. Elynia, I am before your eyes at last after so many childish years dreaming of a dripping hero's frame emerging.

This is the town you saw when you came up from the network of graves. And darkness came a regretless sun setting and filled the claws of cherub corners down the closes, clutching frightened chests. Vagrancy manifest in the forgets of the night. You would not illuminate the underfolds of your curfew, till over the seeds of an infant secret you kept from me, that lay and wait or waste. Its seeds will grow despite what lies beneath. This wind had teeth, and an appetite for you, moaning into the holy vocal warmth of your cord. Forcing forward blasphemy of any stripe. Spilling from an extended hand with a chinging cup, open and blunt, jutted in front of you. The mouthy hole babbled profusely in your face. You could not distinguish the hand form the change from the cup from the hand that receives. Thick smoke choked the rough holder whose hacks and coughs sputtered the jingle of loose change.

Coming the other way, a man who looked like he made fleeting love rubbed a coin between his thumb and forefinger until it grew hot in his pocket; made it homeless, passed, inherited hand-to-hand. Its value remained unequivocally, which equivocated it nothing. You hurried under a flying flag. Its fluttering colors traced deep, root deep, the baton on which to twist and untwist. A flag, cries flies flaps and cracks in the wind and commands, translucent to the sun, becomes tatters.

I am only dumb stone courting nothing, lodged in this bastille. I don't want to leave you.

Growls from the traveler's stomach interrupted his memories, and he ducked below to eat a can of beans just like the one from yesterday and the day before. Stroke by stroke, his tiny folding can-opener tore into the metal. It held to the side of the can with a small peg, and as he twisted, it thrust a dulled, curved blade downward, releasing an odor of bacon and maple syrup. He stood in the galley, spooning at the cold beans in the can and coaxing them to flow. Then, through the thin slit of a side hatch, an immaculate glimmer like a long bone peered out from the hilltop, seized by the gold brilliance of the setting sun's low angle. The traveler looked beyond the town to the slopes above it, beyond the darkened stone of the exposed and simple monuments. At the peak of the lumbering hill, the corner of a brilliant bleached-white wall peeked from the greening overgrowth. It looked like an ancient fortress. Mostly hidden. Its winnowing slumbering notion of violence undressed.

The can of beans waited in his motionless hand. The spoon stood at attention in the half-frozen slurry, a center to the ragged metal halo. But the traveler left the meal in the basin of the sink and went above. The view was little better than through the narrow hatch. His searching eyes found again the brilliant white of the structure wreathed in a forest of enlivening buds and new thorns of wild roses. If he had passed through a week or two later, the white would have been hidden by Spring's growth. But the earth was still stripped from the ravish of winter and glimmered its bones. The white stone entreated him, promising a perfecting distant origin far older than any of the town buildings lower down the slope of the hill. The elder truth crowned the summit. The age of the walls intrigued, and a desire to discover their protectorate began to take him. But it was not their age alone that fed determination; it was their mystery.

The traveler had visited the town as a devoted offspring, who heard the tales of unknown fathers

113

who bled this ground. Searching for their incarnation, he discovered this town like hundreds of others along the canals, pandering the abused beauty of eroding steeples and stone faces, profaned by their future. But beyond, above, glowered the ramparts of perhaps a more ancient struggle. His hunger for anything less fertile had deserted him: the traveler wanted the longest strand of human survival striving, a taproot nourishing the entire length of his life. He braved a promised mirror of himself deeper in the past. That upturned image origin, unearthed pale stone in the waiting darkness. Submerged legitimacy—something offspring could claim its own—would shunt from out the depths to his blithe touch, and bequeath its long view of identity. He longed to inherit the race.

Sleep intoxicated him, pulling back toward the cramped cabin, the narrow berth. He laid down, eyes again shifted restlessly, this time beneath two white sickles circling through the canting hatch. A shiver under the cold blanket.

Morning came soft and anticipatory through the portal. On archaic fields, in the old world, the sun rises slowly, teasing color from the stark night. The sky cracked like an eggshell, and the yellow yolk of heaven burst out in empathy. First light fractured the dreary haze of dreaming history, aching with a sweet discord to investigate the ruins above. The traveler stole onto deck with quiet balance and padlocked the companionway, bounding down to the dock. He passed through the town like a ghost, seeing no one.

Even the bakers were still hidden in the rear of their shops with their ovens.

A serum of light like pale coreopsis hinted at women dressing behind flower-print shades, or hard-boiled restaurateurs prepping their kitchens. He progressed upward through the town, passing its narrow, frigid alleys where the sun did not reach the fusty stone. Ascending staircases beckoned, higher. On the last cross-street of the town a dirt trail broke off, into the wooded slope, where locals climbed the steep spine of the mountain.

The path wound arduous. White puffs of exhale chased him like nagging children, but the exertion and warming day made him sweat. He had dressed for the cold morning, wearing bright red foul-weather gear, a long hooded jacket with overalls for sailing in heavy rains. He stripped off the jacket and hung it from a broken branch of a skeleton tree, to pick up on the return. He mopped his brow with a wool hat and left it with the jacket. The sun grew higher with his first hour up the mountain, and the air continued to warm. The distance was greater than expected. His damp long-sleeved shirt, checker woven of off-white cotton, clung tightly as he squirmed out from within and left it spread upon a rock to dry. Pants rolled up past his knees, he breathed deeply and trudged toward the next bend in the path. After a second hour, heaving and shirtless under suspenders, he stumbled upon the corpse of a thousand-year-old fortress. A boot caught one of the tumbled rocks of an old wall while he looked about in wonder, and dirt smeared his damp, exposed skin when he fell. His chest stung where the ground opened flesh, red nestled in the black dirt.

Thick stone walls knit a chaotic maze in the brow of the mountain, their white half-buried from time. The ragged ranks of stone surrounded a core, where they once preserved a sanctuary of hope against the oncoming storm. The traveler stood in the dissembled center, hoping in the walls. Earth had invaded all the empty spaces. He imagined the network of passages snaking through the ground below, their opulent mosaic floors. How high had the walls been; how deep were the archaic chambers. What lay buried in the secret recesses. He relished the isolated speculation of the ruin, preferring it to the obviousness of the town.

A system of earthen-work ramparts surrounded the interior ruins, terraced and braced by more walls of stone. He walked the periphery to discover that they were the ramparts visible from the boat. He puzzled over them. Assailed them. He sought to pierce the stones together and rebuild the ramparts in the riddle of his mind. His keen eye was sharper than any weapon against which they defended. Amongst the terraces immediate to the central ruins, he discovered a set of stone stairs leading nowhere: their descent buried, their assent plummeted abruptly from the toppled walls. A pair of half-moons was worn deep into each stone step.

He squatted, face inches from the stone, longing for a lone touch, to make contact. It looked porous and rough, aged skin tender and loose. It reflected his breath back onto his extended neck. Observing the brutal coarseness he thought of an old invalid man. Mind wrecked with time, unable to shave. Stretch the loose skin taut to draw the razor. The scraping as he pulled the blade, and the exhausted human smell of cut hair tickling inside his nose. He thought of an old man jutting a vulnerable chin square as the stone, frowning at him as in a mirror. His stale breath kept coming back over his skin from the stairs.

A river flows my touch to you: a current arching across generations, an eternity waiting silently and overgrown with misuse. Touch me in the relics I slough off, merciless things I have seen, that you cannot know though you should. Elynia, touch me, the hypocrite in the stone, so hard and so enduring, still vulnerable, conquered, eroded, ravished. And aging, just like you.

He felt the stubble of his own beard. The sun had risen over the new town across the river, casting its bright streaks of light onto the immaculate walls before him. Examining the stairs the traveler felt a ruin inside, all his honor and faith that had slowly been stolen from him, leaving a pragmatic intellect, fortress of his mind. He felt camaraderie with the ruins, a beautiful destroyed past. A heap basking in the early rays. A slit of illumination managed a path through the thick trees and fell across the stairs before the traveler.

The stone was bright as he had seen from the boat—bleached from its long exposure to the sun.

He burned to touch it, like touching the hero he dreamed. He reached out a feckless hand, five fingers limpid with all the world he had seen that yet failed to teach its meaning; his darkened skin was a sharp contrast to the stone. He hesitated within the sunlight, daring to profane something venerable.

I praise creation that I am at last silent, content to be a skeleton, not an icon. You may bury me alive with your progress. I won't haunt you; I won't deride you. I am the progress that allows you to bury me. Constantly hurried along the mystic morning, the disproved belief, the forgotten sacrifice, and I lately have found myself tired.

His arm cantilevered over the stairs. He resonated with the strength that allowed him to reach and to hesitate at once. To cantilever without crumbling. The stairs waited, begging for his touch, suspending him in their helpless immobile stare.

Brawling labor for you, hungry capstan, turning with the lanky footfalls of languished man. Dried body, stony center, waiting in the decay and earth, empty calabash after its last draught. May I be so selfishly selfless. As coldly elevating. Up. These stairs lead up, up draft from remote labor of eyes like eyes, jaws like laws. Up the conquering standard. Up the execution victim. Climbing these pure stairs from out the dirge of antiquity. Up out of the muck and mud. Climb, damn it, climb! I come to seal you in my belly.

His thriving fingertips sparked on the rough step, like stone on stone—contact that spanned generations. The awed press of his palm tingled with the gritty hardness that seemed to disintegrate beneath his touch, cooing to him about the tall embankments and the stairs losing their faces and memories to the rain. While his face, in the onset of adulthood, had just become mature. Feeling something primordial, outlasting his beginning, made the traveler a predicate of the world, an afterthought of struggle. He had not once been hungry enough to be human. The scattered walls convened with him, stoic bones of a violated grave.

Feet half in the trench, growing out of silence and dust of time. I am bolted across the splint of spirit, sulk for satisfaction, bolt shut door of ruin against the coming. A childhood of lark darkness. Singing of eternity wrought and wrestled from immunity. The empty lust. The empty, empty lust reaching further back in time for an object to desire. An early lullaby to comfort me into coming sleep. You are not alone, it has always been like this.

But after the climax of the stairs there was little else to touch. Time, the conqueror, had been lazy to leave any testament at all. Or maybe time was not yet finished. Or maybe the fortress was unworthy of its destruction. The traveler's hand withdrew as he stood. It was time to go; the hike was long; many miles of canal waited. The trail that led up the mountain beckoned. As he traipsed away in irreverent hurry, his fingers brushed along the face of a brilliant wall, causing loosed sand to rain down, spilling like the side of the stone opened. Reminding him that even these white stones were dirty, sooty, vile, and once men had bled upon them.

Desolation is such an intricate ruin, asleep in the harmony of guilt and purity. Repose in the ruin; exhaustion reposes in its ornateness. Its scale numbing, detail sublime, and all of it as failed as bloodlines. Cradled by vast and exquisite slumber. A stubborn gift. Supplanted not by ruin but by the ornament of ruin. I do not want to hurt in the face of a gift.

He picked his way down the spine of the hill towards the town, shielding his eyes from the sun. It was more difficult walking down the slope than up it, because he had to descend carefully over the rockier sections. Budding trees whispered above him in the soft spring winds. He felt long and tall, as if his feet still rested on the ramparts and his body twisted its iterations through the dark, the war, and now the malnourished peace. Jacket, shirt, and hat waited warm and dry on tree branches. He slipped back into his shirt before entering town. Descending the stairwells of the town, his feet were quick, nearly tripping. He was late. He was too late.

There was the plaza that ran next to the dock. The bells of the town kept silent, the old stone tables in the plaza were all empty, but people moved about the square. He bustled through, making for his boat. But along the river a growing throng of street merchants were setting up tents to sell their wares to tourists. They were a fat, opportunistic, bastard-looking bunch. Scruffed abject faces and wrinkled clothes. Nonetheless, the clothes were expensive, which made their sloth the more sumptuous. Even without speaking, his attitude and looks betrayed him an interstitial foreigner millandering in their midst. They closed on him naturally, a synched noose. Their grotesque wide grins overtook his vision. They wanted him and what they could get out of him, ignorant boy. The traveler was surrounded.

He spoke their language and understood what they called to him.

"Don't just walk by, sir. I have fine silk scarves. The finest. Even earrings, for your lovely at home . . ." The silk laced with rough fingers caressed his flinching cheeks, feeling like water that could drown.

"I have the best coffee, tea, and spices." The ignorant man shoved boxes under his nose. They smelled only of balsa wood, not their contents.

"Sir! I have a deal for you, just for you," he was jittery, "no one will beat it."

"Souvenirs. Take something back for friends, a little something to remember your journey." He couldn't tell what was in their hands, but they were reaching for him on all sides, the mob pressing in to devour him. In the whole open square only this one knot of flesh boiled around him. The merchant's yells echoed from the enclosing buildings. The traveler did not want to be touched; their jagged hands and teeth hurt like the hard splinters of his remaining half-mast. In their grip like the unrecoverable mast lay at the bottom of the sea, giant wasted sail undulating in the current, a beautifully surrendering calamity.

I love my tatters.

"Don't bother with those street scams!" a shopkeeper called to him from a store behind him, "they're all a pack of cheats!" he said. "And liars! You come into *my* store for good deals," and he bowed to the shop's doorway.

"Give her the world, yeah, give her a real pretty ending," yelled a voice with a supple tenor. The traveler whirled and ran for his boat.

I signed off the silk hide of that lust with an X. Convicted myself to put flesh on the stony bones. Held tight through the rust and weather. Passing the time since my ruin. Is there no scansion to stop me tumbling into racing black. Blot out the market on my soul. Serve my wares on the barrel in the pale blue storefront beyond the shadow of the gallows. The stairs of my eyes—nothing more than diamonds and harlots of lost souls.

With the ease of routine he uncleated the heavy lines and threw them onto the boat, leaping onto the deck in a bound. The merchants goading calls of surprise and laughter diminished behind him. The boat drifted slightly from the hurried tramping on board. He rushed to leave, trusting the fenders and empty slips to keep the boat from danger while he started the engine. He unlocked the hatch over the companion way to get at the ignition. Fumbling with the scored metal, he thought of the bolt that once secured the door of the ramparts. Under siege, he wondered if it held.

The siege sleeps now where once I heard footsteps rushing down the stairs into the safety of the rampart arms, charging down into my shelter. Sleep surrounds me. The loci of the skeletal embrace. Night rolls me up in soft tonguing words. Closed up. Self-centered; centering in the ruined world. A lovely bolt holds my door. Shut mouth. Suffering red dawn. Lock me in so it can never be late enough. I outwait time imprisoned in a dream, floating half-awake.

I won't close my eyes, Elynia. Won't sleep. Too tired. Too lonely. Bolt shut the promise in your glance. The glance I'm told I resemble. Click of metal as I turn the knob in the pale phosphorescence under the glow of galley light. See the sinking imperfections I have acquired in my wait. Here are my seams—by morning I'll be transparent. Tired tissue. In blanket isolation, streaming down my veins. Pale blue beneath light skin. Idle. Image. Idol. Everything looks like everything I never had.

The engine warmed only moments as he coiled the lines, their rough braid thick in his fists. He hurried to prevent the current from catching and spinning the boat. He threw the engine into gear just as the bow started to fan across the river. The prop churned; the town, the fortress, the merchants slipped behind him like so much water. The pumping of his heart began to subside, and he stripped off the sticky smell of the smothering overalls. Underway once again. The wind cooled him, shaking off the town he had wished to see all his life. He wanted the flowing river to push it into the past, time to devour it and relegate it to

123

another traveling story. The sun blazed, reflecting on the water, and his skin bared again to the burn.

A final view captured what was still visible of the ramparts. The exposed stones bleached whiter, season upon season, as punishment for their exposition, he supposed. Those stones buried below the earth remained dark, away from the sun, ones that had crumbled to avoid the glowing judgment. There was no inequity among those exposed; all stone lightened, purified by remoteness of perspective. The traveler's distancing made the white seem even more immaculate. Without the bleach of judgment, the stones would not have been bright enough to be seen by the traveler. The sun claimed its own, marking the province of its unblinking eye. Meanwhile, it heaved at the opposite color of the traveler's skin, arm over arm, winching one shade closer, closer, darker as tightening mainsheet clicks following the straining drum. The olive of his skin like the foliage hiding the wall—one break and he would bleach the same.

I am the extirpate culled into your living fortress. Coiled fetal within its living shell. Another and another and I go chasing my fathers within reinstated walls. Across the river I see the lights of the old city, rough flickering like the hangman's rope, the chafe on my throat shaving me. As civilized as the rain.

❖

The storm is unique terror, but its nature is not unique. It has an embarrassing secret, tricking gossip through centuries, but will not acknowledge what everyone knows it hides. A premonition, presupposing a beginning. The rain digests its composition, sinking into the earth's pure depths, infiltrating cellars and foundations, crypts, buried relics. The teeming downpour assonates to a dull whimper in which its fear conceals its pain. There is a struggle to not reveal how much has been forgotten, as its muscles ease it to the stomach of the earth, suffering to taste itself in the final moment. Now the power of the storm is merely decorative and its might, annoyance.

Before the storm the world is dry and bright, unsuspecting, paper-thin, glassine. The storm bellows to full stature, billows up to brilliance but, like its victim creatures, learns nothing. After, the world is drying, apologetic, curious. Mortality blushes before the power of the storm and refuses to be bested. Ropes fling over the sluggish brute of cloud, staked into the dirt to secure its fleeting and powerful mystery. The hulking storm lurches and writhes but the ropes hold. It is only water and motion, water and motion, breath, heat and light. It is not deserved liberty. It rains and rains, giving to the softening earth, coursing and courting, driving along the axis of the stakes, pounding into the grave.

The storm ends, a victim of time and place, heat

and breath. It ends for the upturned faces below: mocks dominion, acts out certain ruin. Wide eyes cautious for final falling drops empathize—knowing the feeling of facing one's boundaries. Lashes slack and wither aimlessly as the clouds fade. They cut loose the memory of shape.

Thought I'd find you here, spinning through this oblivion . . .

She was tentative as she entered the gym. Shadowy goliaths of tall folding bleachers rose at equal sides their heavy pale-blue lacquer, blanketing sinister luster. Ahead, a mass of students like herself and other young people talked and swelled in dance at the far end of the court, a squirming knot of flesh like a slow, boiling caldron. A stage rose behind them, wrapped by a tight-lipped, velvet curtain. On the stage, the man she was looking for. The trumpet player stood for a solo; hips twitching, feet stomping, shoulders dipping, disjointed and random and primal. His fingers raced over the valves; disheveled shirt wet with sweat, tails untucked. It hurt her to look at him. Looking at a future can hurt like a distant and happy past—when each is inaccessible.

Every month there was a social like this one, when young people came from miles to meet and hear the bands. Tonight's was sponsored by the big chain grocery store that had recently moved into town, and a few local civic clubs. Friends in her community college brought fliers for the event to post in the school hallways. There were rich kids at the social, and farmers, too, from the little towns up north that had only a diner and a gas station at their crossroads. They all felt younger than they were, because the event was in the local high school gymnasium.

The trumpet player took his seat after his solo. She bowed her head as his body lowered, to examine her own body. Her black flats for dancing with bows that hinted at ballet slippers. Her bare, precocious ankles and calves and knees. Her favorite dress, a black wrap with a bow tied in the front and lapels at its v-neck. It flowed soft and delicate around her thighs. She looked at her narrow hips and feared she was too thin. She wanted her breasts to be larger. She did not notice the curious boys staring at her as she smoothed her dress and patted her short hair styled close to her head with berets.

Her dress swayed as she inched forward shyly. His hands twisted over one another and locked their fingers, arms stiff down her front. A glint came off the earrings she had borrowed from a friend; she did not own any. The cool air of the gym grew heavy with moisture and heat as she approached the dense group of dancing bodies. Boys shook the sloppy chunks of their wet hair, whirling and twisting with their partners. Beneath her feet, the prized wood court was protected under large blue vinyl tarps. High school boys had been called out of fifth-period Biology earlier that day to haul out the tarps and prepare the gym.

From the edge of the crowd, she surveyed those in attendance with the cunning spark of her gray eyes, struggling to appear as though she was not looking but confidently waiting. But now that she was in sight, she did not want to stand in one place too long. She pointed her toe, dragged its tip along the ground, a long fine line of her leg like a compass making an arc in front of her other foot.

Then she stepped, with a hop. "Don't move like a child," she thought, and circled the crowd until she presented herself before the stage. In a lag of the beat, the stumbling crowd exhaled exhausted, like it would collapse. She could smell the liquor on their breath; the young men hid flasks in their pockets. In the brief silence as the trumpet player stood again, rain hammered down on the metal roof of the gym. She wiped a tingling drop answering from her ear— she had to run inside from the car. Then came the electric notes, clear as church bells but gritty and sensual. His cold blue eyes in pinpoints burned their chilling flame into the vacant shadowed heights above the crowd. Sounds of rain subsided below the music geminating in her direction.

Thought I'd find you here, spinning through this oblivion. You are unlike your riotous creation. I came to seek you in the pale fits of tender love. First, I searched the empty hallways and silent lockers, all the places we never conversed. Now I come to you where you are known, where you are popular. Where you rest by yourself on the bleachers, alone, pretending to savor individuality. Sulking, you call out—come to me. You call me without words. You call me, without sight to startle my admiration, without requital to acquit me.

David Michael Belczyk

She drank him in from her secret seclusion. He, buried in the impulse and impasse of the tumultuous notes. She thrived on his pulsing soliloquy, moving like a slick arrow through her little body. She listened, hopeless. She longed to be his addition and to add him to her gentleness. To know him. To seek him. To find him.

The silence of your unwilling beauty enthralls me. You glow and fade. Your racing hope is my racing heart. Your surrender is my wanderlust. A departure and destination. Heavy upon you, I will be the royalty of your tourniquet. I navigate the accident of you circumlocution, wrapped so tightly round, tripping, tearing. To begin and end with your sleep: I am made the whole intricacy of condemned flesh. Find my piercing eyes and bring me one kiss. One kiss. One. Kiss.

How should she let him know her. As they hid in their parents' basements, for the first time discovering how hard each of their hearts can pound. Surprise. Or in the sunlit field behind her house, overflowing with wildflowers. They could hide in the hollyhocks and black-eyed susans, their springtime seeking perspective of what there is to be found. But one kiss only. Cradle his head in the sunlight and envelop in the heavy smell of pollen learning his heart.

The song ended and startled her dreaming. A voice spit from the speakers, parting the seductive volume as the players sauntered to the stage wings. Laughing couples kissed and groped their way into a bank of faces watching the stage for what was next. A thick rustle of skirts when flirty girls kicked their heels at their bullish lovers. "We're gonna have a short break from the music, and instead we're gonna have something a little out of the ordinary. Something special," the voice said satirically.

A tall man in a tuxedo entered stage right, pushing a dolly of folded chairs. He wore a huge fake smile that said, "I'm here to entertain you, and I get paid for it, but someone else should be pushing these chairs." He tried his best to float onto stage lighthearted despite the anchor of the dolly, but he walked authoritatively, like military. In fact, he had been with the police for years but gave it up after arresting too many people that he thought were innocent. Having no other skills, he attempted his childhood dream of being on stage. But it was hard to lose his old mannerisms. He still looked at audiences with an interrogative scowl. His shoulders, still hulking despite their atrophy, fit tight in the slender tuxedo. It was the largest size available at the local magic shop. His recently stretched shoes squeaked awkwardly, as he arranged the chairs, smiling on. Languid applause bubbled up from the audience and its echo rolled throughout the gym.

He looked into the crowd. "I'm going to need ten volunteers to get up here and join me," the tuxedo grandly orated, grabbing ahold of the angular microphone stand. His voice was weak in the large space after the volume of the band. He reddened, realizing that the microphone was not present at the top of the stand. A thief in the audience snickered loudly. The tuxedo set the stand aside and repeated himself more boisterously. A few hands poked up timid and cautious from the crowd. He called them out with great excitement, as though they had had all eagerly shot up at once. He preened like a hungry predator after the volunteers, or like a cocksure teenager, booming his voice. That would prove his mettle to the fool who stole the microphone. Each volunteer took a chair after ascending the stage. The rusty joints fought but eventually widened their jaws. The tails of the tuxedo bustled between volunteers and arranged them into a semicircle facing the audience. The group was seated.

"Thank you to our brave volunteers. You may be wondering what you are all doing up here." He addressed the audience and paused. "Well . . . are you all ready to be hypnotized!" he roared, turning enthusiastically to the volunteers seated before him with a grand sweep of his arm. The crowd clapped reluctantly, convinced now that the social organizers thought them children. One nonplussed man at the far right of the semicircle stood immediately and walked off stage. The deserter melted into the quizzical crowd anonymously. The crowd huddled together, feeling cold in the large space now that the dancing stopped. But the tuxedo began his routine persuasively as he pulled a gold emblem from his jacket and deftly pushed away the empty chair with his foot. He took his position at the hobbled focal of the now askance circle.

"Feel sleep crawling up your spine, unloosening your joints," he incanted, "sleep like the pressure of all history in a sharp point between your eyes, and the pain of the point floats away because you are relinquishing to sleep. . . ."

The stage was rapt with ritual. The participants dangled on each swing of the pendulum; the audience poised, groaning in disbelief. The girl in the black dress swept into the crowd as it approached the stage and watched among the upturned faces. But she looked not at the emblem, or even at its shining, but across the stage wings, to her object d'art. The powerful slate of her eyes followed him as he rocked from one foot to the other, resting from the performance. Trumpet dangled down, dripping humid breath, his creation exhaled into its hard and narrow lungs. He alternated glances between the tuxedo and his collection of sheet music, reclining a waiting lover on the music stand before him.

Look at me.

This is fun and all, but I am not hypnotized.

The tails of the tuxedo lorded over the unfolded chairs, carefully sculpting his performance of obliviousness. The participants began to roam and contort at the whim of his egregious suggestions. A few of them occasionally cracking brief smiles. Errant whispers arose from the crowd, "Oh, they're all just faking it."

"No, I think that one is really hypnotized. Him too."

"I think she is. She's too shy to make *that* up."

133

"No, look, they're smiling!"

I look back over too many loves. Remember each expression, each episode, like every one was intended for eternity. I loved on a selfish stage. Why not leave rather than make a fool of myself. They'll know I've been faking if I do. Maybe I'm good enough to maintain belief if I stay. If I don't want to leave, maybe I really am hypnotized. This is awfully easy.

She watched him jealously from the crowd as he swayed lethargically, wanting his eyes only for her. But the eyes swung arcs of which she was the lowest point, where they moved most quickly and did not pause.

Look at me.

On stage the hypnotized decanted foolish mimicry. Two sat at a make-believe table gorging themselves on air, puffed cheeks fattened by depleted breath, clean teeth striking and grinding their enamel. Two beguiled strangers clasped enchanted hands and danced a bawdy rag to silence in a tangle of legs. One lulled on the floor, rolling over like a catfish in the lunacy of luscious sleep. Another hovered over, acting out the sleeper's dreams, unloading a library of cosmogonies, a conqueror, a demon, a gypsy hunter, a divine lover. Of the last pair, one built a house, hammering imaginary nails into imaginary planks and marking the pitch of the raised roof with his outstretched arms. The other lived inside the house and changed clothes countless times, preparing to go out: a fine suit, delicately piquing a silk pocket square; a brilliant red dress like a flamenco dancer, a little unsteady on the high heels; or no, the rags of a beggar, a leper; a twirl and what would be next.

The man in the tuxedo dropped his emblem. It sailed a golden arc from his pinched fingers as he gasped and struck a shrill metallic note upon the floor, spinning and sputtering until the chain followed and muffled the sound. The crowd squinted, unsure if they had witnessed an accident. A familiar snicker regurgitated. The participants stopped, and one raised his hands into the air and took a self-gratifying bow. A cadre of friends in the audience applauded. The ritual was over. In the hollow bubble of uncertainty that followed, the trumpet player found her eyes. She shone towards him with all her might. A spark leapt exuberant and mysterious from their plain slate. She showed how she could love him.

Elynia, O how I long for your perpetual purity. Now, years after, I still believe in your purity. Your fragile skin that waited a lifetime for me. If only you were more beautiful. I did not know the beauty of purity. I only knew my own beauty. Had you satisfied me, I could have loved you and you could have sanctified me. Do you remember, kneeling in the spring haze upon the weak early blooms, crushing the vulnerable petals under the strength of our embrace. Cradling you as a knell sounded in the distance, scrawling wild on the crisp sky. I shape and mold in its echoing boundaries. In the song pouring from the O of your mouth, rounded belly of the bells. As you push me into the envelope of green smell. Off balance keeling side to side, I jackknife into the mysteries of unsure pursuit. A desperate bearing of self. I am loved only in confidence, coveted in apathy; I am tolerated. I was unworthy of you.

Elynia, how do you carry your beauty. Do you want to pronounce me, you ragged slit-lipped, skance-slipped, caresser of a knowledgeable formation of the mouth. Cant it to come to my kissing fancy. Our rampage of attraction brutalizing its way through ascent. You have produced yourself, dissonant right out of the blind tone of the earth. Right out of the crushed flowers of my innocent field. Look, Elynia, my dress is stained with the colors the petals bled.

"Do you see that girl over there?" said a shining bobble of bubbling femininity to the trumpet player after a show. She lifted her chin to indicate a lonely dancing girl across the room.

"Yeah," he said, and added, "She looks good."

"That's my roommate," came a giggling reply.

"Is it?" He examined the dancer in her sheath: her petite and sinewy body, curved hips swaying and her playful ponytail fanning open as it bounced. Left then right. Left then right.

"She doesn't know I'm talking to you, she would be so embarrassed . . . but she likes you. And she just got out of a long relationship that ended badly. So, I wanted to make it clear that you should go talk to her." She cooed and sighed as she spoke, high-pitched and breathy.

"Should I?"

"You should. And so long as you don't tell her I talked to you, I'll tell you *exactly* what you need to say."

"Okay, tell me."

"I live with her; I know all her secrets. And I happen to know that she has a special phrase she likes to hear. It's quite unusual, I know, but only the right man will say it."

"You think I don't have my own hypnotic words."

"Not these words."

He considered. "Alright. What are they?"

"Well . . . I'm sworn to secrecy," she giggled, "so if you say it, she can't know it came from me. Walk up to her, the whole time staring at her as you get closer, like you're fixated on her. Then take her hand without saying a word. But don't be gruff. And don't put your fingers between hers, she thinks it feels disgusting. Just take her hand gently and tell her she has the most beautiful eyes, like a whole field of springtime flowers."

"*Like springtime—*"

"*Flowers.* That's it. That's what she wants to hear. And, like I said, she's already interested, she just got out of this other thing. So, if you do this right, she could be yours."

"And what are you all about, matchmaker? You're scarily direct."

"I'm just looking out for my friend."

The trumpet player felt like it was a trap, but he knew he would do it anyway, because he wanted to.

"She'll like it?"

"Absolutely," sounding a little cold for a friend. They stood facing one another; he, the taller of the two, looked down at her, swelled with necklaces, tight clothes brimming with fashion. From the corner of his eye he sighted the dancing, swaying prey offered him like a dumb brute victim of his sex. The friend eyed him back, in challenge.

He sighed, "Well, she is beautiful."

"Oh, and one more thing: don't stay around too long. She'll get tired of it. After a little while, ask her if she wants to leave and get a milkshake, strawberry."

She winked at him—one big blue eye, a lake full of hidden intent—turned and wiggled her finely arched back into the sea of cocktails, suits, and dresses. The escapist friend vanished, left him to his work. Music pulsed over him; he was not playing tonight. The rich ruby carpet enthralled him, spilling its ceaseless patterns, tonguing him as he tongued the words in his mouth. The friend spoke to him as though the mere offer was irresistible to him, would conquer him. As if his simplicity could not know any better than to seize. He did not want it to conquer him. He wanted to be free of the tempting, swaying body. But he knew that he was conquered.

He bound himself as he took his first steps toward the offered. The words tickled a bit when they came out, as though he were about to cough, but choked it back in the brittle obelisk of his throat. She was shocked, and wore the imprudence of inexplicability.

But he eased her, improvising like one of his solos—a firm hand on her soft hip, explaining the different flowers that scented the field like honey, the color of the petals they could crush with their bodies, petals humbled by the truer color of her eyes. The music entwined them. But only a few dances, else he would repeat himself—he wanted her to believe in his infinite reserve of creativity. The delicate pink of the milkshakes was delicious. It spread tawdry on her intoxicating tongue. In a dark apartment he misplaced his new-fledgling belief about virginity.

He gazed intently at her—the girl with bright green eyes that flamed without restraint, without mystery, without creation.

I touch the four walls of my fomentation, succumbing to ease, the ease of accepting I had no means of escape. Elynia, imprison me to reveal me, mirror my vanity. I am afraid to think I have no shame. I am afraid that all my love is the same waste of beauty. Elynia, she has several faces—becoming one face. One of the strangeness of time, one of betrayal, one of pride in the face of anguish. Love languishes over the heat of despair, finds breath, clinging to a sullen melancholy years after. Forgotten falsehoods, livid upon my heart made bare, sum up long summer winds off flowered fields. Her most frail face, saddest face, strikes a powerful fear of starved trust. And her new face understands at all costs, must understand, will understand. The last was vanquished in the throws of succulent effort, warming, loving, believing in a lock without a key.

Several faces: misdirected love, sour proof, the burden of time, of anticipation. Bereft each with its self-creation, each bereaved, cast unlucky upon the desirous upheaval that created the void to be filled. A luscious face calls me to the now, a private face, to the future. And laughter, always laughter, into the wounded past.

The storm is a home of echoes. Its myriad looks and sounds, retort retort, coursing florid and frightening. Each scattering peel of thunder equal in undimmed awe, but indistinct, unmemorable. It comes again and again, the same and then the same. And awe becomes the common. Thunder is thunder is. It impersonates, ensnares as it closes in, stifling. It consumes but is not assumed. The storm coughs claustrophobic in the chests of the drenched. Damp smell of repetitive illness. Incongruous calamity ruins itself upon the threshold of dropping pressure and collapses into the throaty lump of the adams-apple. Choleric thunder against any and all assumption. But those listening assume anyway, assume away the spark that caused thunder that caused sound they shall find cause to shed.

MUST I ASK: TO STUMBLE UPON WHAT MAKES ME HATE . . .

The already-criminal opened the front door of his father's rebuilt home wearing a lithe body that inherited his father's toil, and stepped toward the impregnable captors with his hands raised. Shy and vulnerable, his wispy locks licked the gentle breeze through which he emerged an emigrant haze of progress passing. Blurred indiscriminate by the smoke of their commands, he was misidentified, head bowed to the snarling teeth of the immigrant mouths like broken bricks of dying towns. Before the show of order, the already-criminal was only the accumulated fragments of fathers' dreams—his reluctant, lifeless feet sifted through the clattering pieces unassembled. The long line of official force fixed on him, dwarfed by their symbiosis—judgment that made guilt, guilt that made his innocence. He moved toward judgment with perfect slowness, eyes full of fear. They flitted over the stern faces, recognizing men from his father's store. The tangle of his dark black hair lulled into his vision.

A silence gripped the vim hands of order and the two of an innocent, the lulling breeze, hushed trees, sapphire sky, fidgeting weapons, footsteps. The already-criminal's slim figure appeared emaciated, as though he had holed-up starving in his sanctuary. Sunlight threaded a thin shadow struggling into the brilliance that blinded him to his captors. Delivering himself to order as his father surrendered to the town. A father's second version. The attempt of repaired incarnation. The already-criminal felt that he was the only one like himself in all the world, hollowed by gnawing loneliness. The one, among the force, he felt most strongly the relentless knife of loneliness, as his eyes rolled upwards, his raised hands faltered. The officers expected him to have lost his mind, mad from waiting.

I own your sadness, Elynia. Because I cause your sadness. A sadness unnecessary but for my disobedience. A disobedience allowed as the price of love. That I could be like you and force sharp creation infinitely further, sparking through the corpse of time. Weakening age humiliates me. All this long life and all these failures and pain, and I still do not know who I am. Draw back the veil on the inheritance of my suffering so I may know. Make these creases in my captive skin like the rain erodes me into crags. Caress the tomb-like shell where I have been routed by the incessant rain.

We own his sadness. We will never leave. His peace for ours. Order will gnaw at him with chaos, with pain, with starvation, with abuse and neglect. We will bleed him. Give him a stony heart that can master its captivity. One fine piece for a mosaic of need.

The captors looked for any sudden movement, a twitch in the already-criminal's eyes, a nervous mumble out of his mouth, something to disclose the inevitability of his final self-desecration. But the already-criminal stopped with hands raised, poised before them a willing captive, and did not refocus himself—no mumble, no twitch, no desecration. Tackled suddenly from his right side, he was searched, handcuffed, and roughhoused. Three officers lifted him by his armpits, feet dangling, toes scuffing the pavement, before they thrust him down, behind the bars of the wagon with unconditional room like a mother's heart. The dirty smell filled his nose.

I am theirs; they are my misery. By that misery I am given identity. What strange dependency. They guilt me, until my hope shines like gilded greed. The indignant smell of captivity sticks to my sweating face; the stench so strong the taste is on my tongue; savor this humiliation. When I cannot plead the defense of what I am. My dry cotton mouth, dry with the venom of insurrection. Gauzy-dry mouth that tastes the wounds of my captors. My thick tongue slur of a life is suffering words like opulent scraps upon the floor to beggars.

We are his. Our existence amounts to his attrition. It is nothing to have his flesh. His origin is what we need. We will make him come forth with his origin.

He endured his transport in a heap of sweat and jostling bones, unaware of his crime, unaware of his conviction, unaware of the road he traveled into the mysterious future. The already-criminal watched listing dogwoods race past his bars as the driver sang in a bellowing baritone, voice fluctuating as he bounced over the rough road. The driver seemed familiar with the road, a friend of the road, the driver who built the road, named the road, and stepped first upon its hot asphalt diasporas. The car halted. The captors lifted the already-criminal by his steel collar of incomprehension, handed man to man down the path into the prison, buoyed along on the gush of certain guilt. Through the high stone walls, the courtyard and its well, into a darkened inner room like a profaned temple.

A young officer approached him with hypnotic swagger. Intending to lull the already-criminal into submission, he oscillated between compassion and threats. He drug a strike-anywhere match across the leather of a freshly-shined shoe, and the smell of sulfur filled the room as he lit a cigarette. The captors wanted the already-criminal's identity. Feckless questions came like beating upon sand to move an ocean. But identity was not dressed in the proper form to be presented. How could he voice the mystery from which he shot like an arrow. How could he reassemble the jumble of pieces into their shattered mosaic, playing only here and there with shards of separated similar peoples all telling different versions of the same ineffable truth. He spoke himself like a distant, shapeless figure—does it walk towards or away—always a splendor just beyond the cusp of recognition, so the observer must question: perhaps it is I who drift effortlessly.

They stripped off every malnourished felicity. They stripped him. Doused the lights of his eyes under black frock. His heart pumped hard in the labyrinth of assailing doubt, pumping to regain the deficit he shed. Their questions mere quotas between debtors.

What do you know about misery.

I know it is the fruit of my desires.

And what do you desire.

Justification for my fears.

And will you swear upon the distance betweenthe two.

I swear upon my heart laid fallow. It has born, and you have reaped. Now it rests.

"We have a victim who says she's been robbed by some deviant, who helped himself to her little vulnerability, who stole her ability to love. She says it's like someone took her faith, her innocence, her history."

But when his captors accused him, the already–criminal took no oath to tell them what they already knew.

"This is your fruit. Huh. Had to let a good girl have a taste of disobedience. Come on now, we've all seen your muscles from working in your father's store."

I have been too long in this room of lost beauty. I am not frightened of the captivity. But that I should die here in the cold and damp. With knowledge of the cell, I have now known its lust, I have now known its flaws, I have now known its mosaic image of glory. Oh Elynia. Oh necessary wrong.

David Michael Belczyk

From further away, his image seems more complete. But when we test him closely, it examines scattered, an eclectic collection of loose principles. Closer, and it is only a joint of mortar, clinging fast to stainless hope. But we find no identity or innocence. Tell him anything; we must press him to give us a name.

"Haven't I done all that you asked! Why are you taking me back!" But while the already-criminal yelled it was now the captors who stayed silent as they pulled him by his shackles deeper into the pit of the prison, deeper than interrogation, into despair. Mysterious survival awakened within him. And he fought at last, like an animal, uttering cries, not words, twisting and arching his body, flailing his legs that drug upon the rough stone. But he could not stop them. And had nowhere to run had he broken free. The unsatisfied captors deposited the already-criminal into a lonesome cell where they did not visit. They assigned him a number, exercising their prepotency to name him. He shared his numeration with all prisoners, so that his number was different without being unique.

"This is on account of systemic wrongs," they said.

"But I'll be so lonely. Let me have a companion!" he pleaded. But his cries went unanswered.

I am told that outside my close walls the world gives homage to imperfect memory, making pilgrimages to shadows of paradise. A truth like my freedom. While I live in shadows, a persisting memory, a legend that time will swallow. I have only so much patience. I cannot wait forever to know who I am.

Would you give a viper to an infant—a stone to a son who asks for bread. He will be their answer as he denies us ours. Release is out of the question. If we cannot know him, then we must prevent others from inheriting a memory that they will honor like truth.

The already-criminal lay down to sleep in the arms of his consubstantiation of capture, each solemn sinew aching, resonating with undisciplined understanding. If he had behaved like his captors expected, they would have treated him the same. Both sides of the torrential questions intended creation but not what either creates. Wielding a power beyond themselves. The exhilaration of the already-criminal's undisciplined fear made joy from rage, to stand upon flawed completion—to stoop to the flawed complexion—to root spirit in bone.

But the floor was cold where he lay, so very cold against his complexion. Soon his image was covered in sores. The red and white interposed to obscure his identity from the brief judgment that placed his tiny piece amid the mosaic promise of knowing good and evil. His sores like the inception of the promise. He shivered, sweating, on the freezing slime of the floor. He could not stop. There was no one to hear him cry out.

Just one foul question hangs like a dagger on my tongue, its arrogance a weak womb, life giving impatient dyspathy. Its jewel supplicates weakness. We endure it, push, push it like our own casket. Must I ask: to stumble upon what makes me hate, to trip and bash my face on the source of my angst, scowling chip-toothed and bloodied at the source I sought. We are the conquest of knowledge. We have constructed nothing but a constructor—a figment breeding only suckling figments, conditioned to dependency. We shall not stop, even to kill our paradise.

Cowering around the already-criminal, a circle of curious liberators formed the forgotten prostrate figure upon the floor. One of them spoke innocence, in a haze not of recollection but of premonition, the speaker not yet knowing if he was the captor or already the criminal.

"The world is an outlaw state."

A mother leaves her naked infant in the downpour. Rainbow beads stand erect and opalescent on his unblemished skin like pearls. The storm has encompassed his Caanan cry; its promise coalesces the sound of pounding drops. Brow like a wall that wails. Eyes like the tombs of patriarchs, smothered by the expanding black privilege of the infant-killer. Soft nose with a bridge like the house of the first man, wearing new silk. Jaws like jaws, inheriting their fruit. And a mouth like an ark that pours the dust of covenants into the flood.

The new body squirms with potency, potentiality, in flagrant denial of the damp that will end it. A body like infinite potential bodies hiding inside him, hiding beneath forgetting. The storm erodes flesh like stone—slightly, slowly with every storm, until at the end of days remains a nameless heap. Streaking downward curvature, robbing echoes of a genesis, treasured because they were treasured, adored for an importance buried in history. Running channels cut a route more deep and saintly. Steal all monuments.

The rain has no compass. Its direction is singular. It assuages simply, generously when those below ask to melt. The rain hides the face of the infant with its blur of direction, cascades down from his Eden stem, closes his tiny body in its tinier totality, fatal authorship identity to clang along the arpeggios of a soul and tickle his adorable pilgrim feet.

AND THE BOY WAS INTO THE SECRET
RIVER OF SLEEP . . .

A boy in middle school, with a fragile jaw like jaws before, leaned with intent over the leather top of a low children's desk in his bedroom. His brown hair was studiously parted, each small puffy hand pressed into his full pale cheeks, holding up his head as he stared with hypnotic love at the yellowed photograph of a soldier. A timeless and familiar face frozen in nobility, to substitute for faceless time in its impersonal tantrum. A pillow to recline his budding concupiscence. The picture had a sterling courage for which the boy ached, courage which he made a hero, doing his best to adopt it, try it on like antique and formal battle dress. Courage, that roots in perspective. And how the boy had gazed at the picture from every perspective: from his seat on the carpeted floor of the bedroom while doing homework, from the corner where he played by himself as he leaned against the stripped wallpaper and made pictures in the grain of the carpet then brushed them away, from his bed where he lay reading or waking, from the hallway as he entered the room, from the horizon of his rounded shoulders as he left.

A little hand snatched up the picture in its brass frame and polished its glass reverently. There was a smudge on the glass, where he must have absently stroked the beloved face. He returned the frame gently and reassumed his posture, knobby elbows upon the leather, persistent and still as a smudge himself. Not like the smudge on the glass though, oily streak dispatched by hot breath and the sleeve of a uniform cardigan. Like a smudge of his precious hand in the dust on his mother's dining room table. Even a dirty hand still pushes away the dust. Its ever-present, ambient layer becomes apparent through the smudge. Not by the child's fault, but from the tear in the uniform.

A tiny smudge in settled dust, he gazed at one he never knew. The rectangle captive captivated the prescient mimicking face: soft cheeks pudgy braying youth, belaying imitation, hovering both on and beyond the glass. The potential of his youth shone from the ember of his bright summery face, reaching toward lean and muscular life, the virility and action of manhood, right there in crisp uniform. He wished for all the attributes written plainly on the face in the picture: honor, courage, compassion, learning, generosity, honesty.

"The lines of your uniform are so *defined*," whispered the boy, who found relief for his longing only in the picture—clear and captured in its ideal. "I wish so much to be like you." He read and reread the depth of the shallow face. Its depth seemed to extend infinitely behind the beneficent and strong smile.

David Michael Belczyk

A shade of conscience floats below your eyes with dreamy potential. You may hide with me and seek. Not concealed behind my frame but translucent with my gaze. You can lay me face down in homage. You're embarrassed and offer a little humble bow. I lose all stature. Lift me up again. See how I have waited honestly. Place me by the magnificent eye of the window to bleach white in the magnified sun: details of the past faded before undiscriminating brightness.

"How can I be strong like you?" the boy asked, positioning his reflection over the face. He knew some of the stories, how an overseas hero had risen up in his human being and became a great sultan churning and bursting with the heat and sweat and diesel and grease. Who tasted gunpowder every first breath, waking each day with the grit rolling between his tongue and front row of teeth.

Know me now, love. I watched your grandmother sweating over the glasses she washed behind the bar. You know her asbestos hands. Let me carry you away. I told her.

"I know how you eloped," said the boy like he harkened to a plot in a den of thieves. Young surfeit coaxed out the child's spring-tide love. "I read poems by people who loved with abandon. I write them also, to no one. I have not done it yet."

Know me now, love, carrying wounded. I put that poor man's body over my shoulders and he shuddered with speechless pain. I'll carry you to the medics. You'll live. I told him.

152

"I never heard the story from your lips. Where you swam a deep and wide river to warn a town of danger after discovering their communications were destroyed. You warned as many as you could to leave with their lives, and the would-be conquerors marched into a quiet, empty shell. What a broad river it must have been, broader than your fear, I suppose. Is that why you were decorated."

A river like glass. I pressed myself tightly under its surface, looking back. It was a very slim space between me and them, beyond the strong current deceptively reflective. If I'd rescued you, I would hoist you up and carry you over to be safe with me. I'll carry you, love. To put a stubbled, scratchy kiss on your innocent forehead.

"I imagine the way your arms broke the silver tongues of the smooth water. Did you wear your uniform so they would know to trust you. Wasn't the wool sopping wet. Didn't it grow heavy in the water." He stared across the answerless river. A half-smile, worn out of pride alone, reflected happiness amid struggle, but it persisted unwearied in the patience of love. The boy dreamt ligaments of the river's body stretching, springing to life and leaping the void, stroking and kicking arm over arm and leg over leg.

"Those people you saved saw you coming for them; they looked to you and saw only life."

Know me now, love—who never touched this face. Know me in my patience, always smiling. See how you are always accepted by my joy. I am here, across

153

this river; now I am the one waiting for you. I am choking in the breach of history's dry heaves. Oh please, Elynia, gather me in. Store up all the things we threw away, listing lost lives in unrelenting time, lives moldering in value. From euphonic history. Just as, child, your maturity is me—the tiny infant once. You can't believe it.

"I've heard it repeated how you carried a wounded man for seven miles to a medic station. I imagine how he was draped over your back like a sack of potatoes. His wound must have been so hot against your neck. You never told anyone. The wounded man lived in your town, and thirty-five years later he told the story to your surprised brother-in-law at the grocer. By then you were gone. A photograph. Did you look the same as this photo, or were you different when you came home. They say you fought for five years."

Until my dread was a hardened callous. Ever spit on a callous to soften the skin. Rub it brisk after and the tinge will return. Or if it would be days until we'd bathe, I'd douse my hands in the used oil. So they wouldn't rub raw. Or to seal the burns.

"After all that time escaping death, you got a concussion from a careless supply truck. Being hit in the head must have hurt. What about your face. Was it altered. Was it damaged."

The child passed the long hours of the afternoon by writing secret notes he then hid inside the frame, an artifact older than the picture itself. Made of antique brass, the frame glimmered mutedly. Along its sides fine and delicate etchings of thorned vines and flowers entwined and bloomed in endless season. The boy undid the fragile latch at the back and slid his notes carefully behind the picture before sealing it in once again. He imagined with pleasure that the two shared the secret, each of them laughing inside. He loved having a secret across the grave. Language buzzed heavy in his ear like a guiding hand gruffly gripping his right shoulder. Sleepy mysteries winked and nodded intoxicatingly from every corner. He created with his smiling conspirator, then strained with all his might to avoid cracking an unnerving smile and spilling the secret. He was squeamish with the fear of revelation. But the boy held tight and never cast even one beam of knowing from within the ark of youthful awe.

Where did you, what did you, how did you know your own cost. Tell me about the swirling poison of a continent broken with footfalls of liberation. Tell of the sacrificial love of comrades. Raising a shot-through patriotism flagging. Tell me. Just as the tiny flags surround the billboard at the entrance of the train station, whispers fluttering in concert with the headline: "Welcome to our liberators!"

"I won't tell," the boy pledged, "Not now, not ever."

Little questions won't settle down. They nag like an ungrateful child. Confronting me with the horrors of what we had to drink to do. They nag like bashful, bleating inexperience that lives in a dream.

Evening fell on the enraptured boy. The unconsciousness of night held twinkling stars above the child looking beyond his window. He imagined them healing his need for attention, pretending concussion, and imagined them in the slim separation between his eyes and eyelids. Dizzy to descry the sore bridge of his nose, with pain ringing, he closed his eyes before the bandaged distance of the room, winding constellations firmly within snips of cotton. An apprehensive view across the invalid bed to the picture would dress tight the blur of his bound eyes: vulnerable sleep of puberty, the tender eye of the room enclosed around them flickered. And the boy was into the secret river of sleep.

Youth is an autochthonous plot, creeping in brazen innocent passion. Bare shame. The innards of the wriggling dream spilled with alarm. Primordial and androgynous, begotten by its own will, squinting in the glint of its own rays. Swimming through the pane. Elynia, I want the secret.

Matured in the glass, before two sets of eyes— one changed, one unchanging—the boy grew before the picture, ever-fascinated by the frozen moment. It became his fascination to freeze every moment, so he grew to a young man bloated with fantasy and self-remembering relics. The picture turned face down, out of shame, when he indulged himself. And worse even—life was ordinary. He was no one's hero. He despaired that he had sacrificed sacrifice: that the world had changed, and certain dreams and nightmares were no longer possible. A young man— at the brink of the frame loomed a terrible continent, grotesque in etching, brooding and pouring turbulent breath into eddies of frozen brass.

In the chill of autumn in the attic, he said to his mother one day, "These old pictures of the family, they're amazing. I can't believe your uncle still had all these." Looking for resemblances distracted him. He carefully handled the faces in the photos that recorded the long strain of his creation.

"Come look at this. This one is of me and my brothers and sisters, next to the rose bushes behind the house where I grew up." She reached toward him, stretching as far as she could from beneath the heavy box of pictures.

But one photo with frilled edges had already captured the young man's attention. Something suspicious about that face. The romance of his despair remonstrated with pride, searching the confessed, chagrin flesh aglow. No answer came; his eyes searched the wrinkled grey for a heroic self-proclamation. The young man did not see the eager noble face he had memorized. As he gazed in silence, his mother was hurt that he did not receive the picture from her eager hand.

A pensive face mirrored again: weathering skin folded in the dark knit of brows.

"Who's this," the young man pointed with two outstretched fingers at the grainy photograph.

"You don't know who that is." She finally let her cantilevered arm fall.

He saw an aged face fallen with scowl, puffed and confused. Defeated, not ready to conquer. "No."

"Who do you think you've been looking at on your desk all these years."

He inhaled and refocused his eyes, asked to believe something he did not want to believe. It felt like he was about to steal something, fully engaging the wrongness of the act while completing it. Afraid he may have recoiled unintentionally, he said, "That's him."

"Well, after-while, he looked different. You knew, after he came back—"

A disparaging walk back to a desk filled with textbooks and homework landed him again in front of the picture. Shuddering at the face in the other photo, he gazed intently again on those ever-living eyes. This was him. It was the youth the young man knew, recognized. And it was the picture that made up the young man's youth. This is right, he thought. And he rejected the moldering old attic photo for his own youthfulness.

"My God," he said, looking harder at the soldier in the brass frame, unexpectedly afraid. "I must be as old as you are in this picture."

This image grew up before my eyes, while I grew, mending the absence of a cherished hero. I missed you. But growth leads to temptation: to cherish absence more than the hero created. Our embrace reaches me like another's pain that is beyond understanding.

Please don't betray me—give me always your gaze of courageous beneficence. The mending of your face grows deeper and more merciful from within the frame—observing always the corruption of my age without flinching. Your smile is steadfast. Your neediness pumps hard through my fashioning shuddering; I can barely stand the sound. I still wish to be like you. But who is your might—from your own weakness you need me, else you would be forgotten. But look at my weakness. Were I to forget, who would I imitate.

The picture seemed to reply, "When you struggle so, how can I carry you, how can I—O! the ache of my concussive skull. You will not drape across my broad back. Won't fold exuberantly. You don't want to be carried to safety. Why else would you not cry out while anchored by your wound in the mud. I can barely hear you from your savage repose."

But I kept you always.

Mists hung in the portrait of the sky. The weather beautiful in all its moods. The old man looked wistfully through the window glass, dreaming how the ghost of the cold mist might fill his body through his nostrils. His chin jutted outward from his warm collar. He could brave most weather, he thought, feeling the grizzled fragile chin. If the chill would stop shooting sparks of pain through his hollow bones. He inched up from the edge of the bed sheet and turned, his loose grey hair vaguely encircled his head on the pillow. He had laid in bed so long, ill. What to do but roll over again and again, waiting for sleep, for nothing, like a feckless buoy bobbing unnoticed in an endless sea. The staggering monotony is crippling. Rolling away from the window he knew the arc of his sight would again confront his face, a gleam upon the glass, upon the indelible face. Even after a lifetime he still looked at the picture like it was the first time he had ever seen it, resting on the desk, a short but difficult hobble from his bed. His own face was so gaunt, skin weeping in long folds like streaks of rain, burning before the youth, the young fool braying in full-blooded pride, now on the opposite side of the glass. Is this how the old man would finally die then, accompanied by his only companion—maybe wild-eyed with fear before the patient smile.

He labored toward the desk, braided the loose skin of his frail frame into the strong vines etched immortally fresh into the brass enclosure that held the picture. A victim of a lifetime of lost history, lost heroes, lost loves, ultimately led defeated by acid lust, the old man's identity faded like the picture, with time. But their likeness persisted. Bold young perceptions of the face had blurred, but in their stead came the menagerie of the body depicted by the projected face. One that perhaps looked beyond failure. Authorship lingered in the bridges of the noses, the cheek bones eclipsed round and firm, the eyes set wide, and the chin strong. He turned the picture face-down to hide his shame. New-found and newly late.

I never abandoned the vigil of your hope. I'm pronounced by imitation alone. Your promise of imitation. Have I been brave. Have I learned all that I could. Sought tirelessly to make you proud. But I did not recognize your face, could not find your ideal in the world beyond the frame. Imago engraven, immortal flowers and boughs in the brass laud the transept of passage. Unwelcome liberation. If only I were a picture and not a play upon reflecting glass. Perhaps another could learn from me, instead of my pity, founded upon an imitation, faced with the original.

The downturned frame exposed its clasp at the back. The old man stared at it, and smiled contemplatively. Ragged fingertips traced his pursed lips as he inhaled dreaming. When *was* the last time he opened that latch. The gnarled fingers extended cautiously, felt the hinges as though expecting a frightened heartbeat. Overwhelmed with curiosity for the old argot, he flung the clasp open. A little note folded in threes waited there, embossed with his name. His first stationary set. Head leaned over the supine, spilled frame, he breathed deep, wanting to inhale the escaping wisps of his child's breath trapped with the note. He picked it up, remembering the precious little hands that were the last to touch. How they had changed. The brittle note yielded gingerly.

Yesterday I sat on the floor in my room and traced hearts in the carpet surrounding me, then wiped them away. I was sad and don't know why. I'm a little sad yet today, but not so much. I miss you.

Life had seemed so long and painful, but now seemed over in an instant. Stroke-numbed hands scrawled in wobbly letters, "still," beneath the fledgling child's script. It was too difficult to write all he wished: I am still sad and still miss you. The old man refolded the note and returned it to the frame. He stood the picture. Beheld the man. Infinite steel blue sadness washed over him buzzing in his solitude. Lost in a hero made without contact, loved without sight, just a long-glowing filament, pictured into the benevolent distance. The picture itself stared into the sepia cartouche. Crisp in his military uniform, a gentle smile for "mom and dad," penned in the corner.

Hardly a form, leering a descending melody. At your negative in outlines distended. Elynia, carry my crippling potential. Converse conversant concaving. Gather brilliant color in the void. Draw back a veil and peak down over the ledge of your gauzy dry mouth. A feast in such resolution must be disassembled, must be fractured. Line severed from line, from hand from mouth, light from light. It is dismissive parquet. The background of your gaze is overthrown by the current of your stillness. How about it, make all this hard for me. I am immobile in splitting ache. Your bandages are all I have inherited.

"Folded up in a worn-out shirt, I am forcing myself back through the buttonholes. Against entropy. Folded, wrinkled, pressed flat within finer creases. My shoulders bend underneath the stench of this old shirt. I have the stars in my hand. My bandaged concussion now lurks in my memory. I have stars in the starch of my collar. A stained collar—starched stiff and bleached. I am the collar stays—stuck through the constellations of my gullet. And the night is so famously red."

A choir of un-honed harmony strikes a celebratory chord of sadness. Drunken, braying worship. Inside the storm it resonates, brewing. The storm scowls rumbling, its face engaged with its own disgust. The blanketing sound unlike the joy of the drunk men's choir at the top of its lungs. The cloud darkens, tumbling down the declension of the sad chord. Scuttles like a choke in the throat of manhood facing the storm from its adolescent trench, eking out its own magnificence at the expense of the thunder. It strikes up and crashes. Pours like honey, drawing itself down in one sweet, stretching strand. Melts on the ground. Tastes like conclusion.

For their countenance, their folded texture impenetrably rising, the clouds seem terribly empty. They sing out a melancholic bass that requires a great hollow to match its amplitude. The thunder roars from deep in the vague and formless gullet, crying out from the open throat of the earth.

They could feel fingers of peeling paint hook into their dresses like a prying miser . . .

"Hey! Don't kill that all yourself."

"Hurry up; pass it before someone comes down."

The flask broke from the teenager's lips; the hollow gulp of a kiss echoed in its belly.

"That's good," came his roguish retort, throat burning. He coughed, face quivering.

You speak in memories, child's lessons I have outgrown, and it's emptiness I am that resonates you. A masquerade of betrayal, echoing corpse innocence. Down in the frozen copse of your soft memories, uprooted by my foolish and perpetual adolescence. I cry ice like breaking glass, like splintering limbs, cold streaks run the length of my face. No words fill my vacant space that longs to ring with your kiss. Don't startle me instead with the sound of my voice. No retaliation, no supplication. I will be your solitary loving lament. I'm self-affliction that way. There is no self-giving thus to despair.

Three shaggy heads crouched in the darkened boys' locker room at the back of the school basement. They scuffled about on the brick floor as they passed the flask, enclosed by the tall metal obelisks scored and dented with age. Their whispers echoed off the high ceiling and hard surfaces. One was a virgin, which the others knew though he had never told them. One had recently had his second virgin, and the girl gave him a scarf that she wore in her hair, now tied tight around his wrist. The third was never interested in dating, though he had some opportune importunity; all he ever wanted was to be military and find himself in dangerous situations. He wore a gold chain around his neck, to appear as tough as he felt, despite the remnants of a childhood lisp. A few minutes before, the scarved hand stole the janitor's key ring from an old square nail over a dirty slop sink near the cafeteria, and eagerly telegraphed success to the others down the hall. Then they made for the lockerroom—locked themselves inside.

Meanwhile, the school congregated in the muddy practice field a quarter mile up the hill behind the classroom building and surrounded by ancient pines. Students milled about aimless in a mass that smelled of puberty, conversing in huddled groups and cliques of friends. The girls showed off their skimpy skirts, legs and lipstick. Tall and short, heavy and slim, cocked their budding hips and thrust their chests as they prattled about, embarrassed and discombobulated. Ready to tease and play with the lesser sex, as they were told they should. Sweaty boys sported their new, patchy facial hair, sauntering ragged shoes in the dust beneath the bleachers. Excited to cuss at one another. Secreting cigarettes. An indiscriminate cadre of neutral blues, grays, and browns—dulled and homogenous as the weak male examples for their emotions. A cynical group of teachers huddled apart, in a corner of the field, one-upping each other's complaints about their schedules, spouses, the administration, and the shoddy work their selfish students passed off on them. A few also snuck in a cigarette.

The assistant principal stood lone before the inattentive seething crowd, "The Twelfth Annual Powder-Puff Football Game will begin in fifteen minutes."

The swarm began to settle on weathered wooden bleachers that creaked with slothful exertion. The boys in the basement could not hear the announcement over the loudspeaker, but instinct told them they had made enough trouble and they should get to the field. Each forced one final shot of whisky into their queasy stomachs. The virgin rinsed the flask thoroughly in the sink, using hand soap. He imagined his mother washing dishes in the sink, and tried to be as thorough. The flask slipped slender into a school-colored gym bag; the boys ferociously chewing gum to banish the burning alcoholic fume.

The boy with the sash produced three old cheerleading uniforms. The boys wiggled as they slid into the slender skirts. It was traditional, for powder-puff football, that girls played in the game and boys performed the half-time show in place of the cheerleaders. Earlier that day the three had investigated available uniforms, and an hour later, during French, the assistant principal threw down a heap of the largest, oldest, most dust-ridden cheerleading uniforms he could recover from the depths of the labyrinthine basement. One-piece uniforms, skirted and sleeveless, made of heavy brown wool. They had moldered down there with the memories of transforming women who lamented that they were no longer slender, innocent, energetic. Here and there clung a strand of brunette or a ringlet of gold. One could not help but wonder what those bygone girls thought they would become when life was simple, and their bright hope-filled voices playing in the afternoon-lit autumn leaves was as pure as faith itself.

Now the three boys parted old memories with the insistent arrows of their bodies, shimmied into the ungiving wool and managed to get their arms through. But then they could not zip up the backs, even halfway, leaving an open slit that closed in a V from their shoulders to the small of their backs. This slit allowed the only motion within the cocoons.

"Hey, your fly's down," joked the gold-chained boy about the zippers as they pushed each other. The slick tile floor waited for the slap of flesh if the unsteady fools should fall.

The three hurried out, carrying the bag with the flask and their clothes as they hustled through the locker room and up the two flights of stairs to the school's east hallway. Rushing for the exit, the sashed hand clutched the stolen janitor's keys. Six harry legs in awkward skirts were twenty feet from the exit when they heard the assistant principal's feet pounding down the hall, back for a sweep of the school before the game. A frenzy of sash and chain and skin ducked into a cavernous empty classroom. All together, they froze in position, hardly breathing.

The immense authoritarian frame lumbered past the cracked door. Large, muscular legs bulging beneath athletic shorts, shoes heavily slapping the terrazzo floors. Keys jingled with each monumental step, until the repetitive *ching* faded around a corner. The boy with the sash quietly deposited the janitor's key on a desktop; there was no hop of returning to its nail. Then, plunging through the door, the boys dashed for the exit, pushing each other in a flurry of skirts. The assistant principal whirled around, craning a thick neck and scowling, just missing the culprits, who burst from the stale shadows into dazzling cool autumn brightness. Lanky and proud, flags of brown and gold wool and paleness paraded towards the field, uniforms tight and nearly ripping.

Elynia, I was asleep. You are blood rushing back into my numbness. Fingers, limbs would not bend when a scalding poured through my arteries. Burst from placental memory. A thousand needles prick my joints to move. I become supple with the burn of awakening. Rush of womb. Swaddling nourishing. Spark me to life. Elynia, quickening.

Three shaggy heads poked up over the horizon of the hill and scrambled into the shadows at the periphery of the field just before the teams were about to charge out. The boys hid beside a long vacant and boarded-up concession stand, not yet wanting to reveal themselves. They had final preparations remaining. As they leaned against the concession, they could feel fingers of peeling paint hook into their dresses like a prying miser staring lustily. The pops and squeaks made them feel queasy as they slid down the wall to the cool grass. Splayed legs ignorantly opened their skirts.

The girls' teams, wearing old home and away football jerseys, trotted to midfield from secretive huddles behind clumps of pine trees at opposite end of the grass. Though the game was flag football, each girl had a full set of pads and a helmet, also from the school's basement. They advanced like warriors, shoulder to shoulder in the oversized pads. The girls loved pretending to be boys, especially pretending to be the boy they crushed, or thought they loved. Controlling the mysterious dark river ever emanating in that confident body—a lock to tame and commune with its flow, a dam to harness its power. And though the girls were crass themselves, behind the grill of the helmet they felt no taboo, that nothing was wrong, only more or less correct. The soft and slender bodies sensationalized the sudden feel of donning physical prowess. Breathy voices joked about it in low tones while getting ready, doing their best to mimic what boys must say about girls when they were not around to hear. The more developed ones had trouble fitting their breasts beneath the pads.

The teams swarmed the field preparing for the first play. Though they had made a fine entrance, confusion reigned before the first snap—the assistant principal had eliminated kickoffs to simplify the game. Most of the girls never watched football, and the school had not had a team in decades. A familiar must pervaded the freshly discovered jerseys dancing again about the field—but this was one of masculine dreams that escaped in to the air. A must of stale hopes for power or wealth or fame, to be a senator, a sports champion, a CEO, to swoon women, to protect a loving family. Lost dreams of men who went bald young, with wrinkled faces and paunches because they grew up too fast, mad with desire. Who looked back on a few big games in a few short seasons when they strode in those uniforms like conquerors. And now there was only work, endless tedium, uncharitable women who did not admire or appreciate them. And court dates for domestic violence charges always lingered, because alcohol was the only affordable escape. The old wool jerseys, stiff with this musk, loved the change from muscular chests to creamy, delicate bellies. Girls felt the jerseys' scratchy wool riding up their skin unusually, excitingly.

How I cried when you were born. Someday you'll find someone who loves you, just as much as you love me and I love you. And I will love you forever because I gave birth to you. I will always believe in you, and I will always forgive you. Nothing can erase our bond. But one day a beautiful woman will come into your life, who will care for you and adore you, and you will give your whole life, even all your pain, freely in devotion to her. And that's how I'll see you in heaven.

Boys in the crowd tried to identify their girlfriends on the field but could not because of the thick pads and helmets. They examined what sexual curves could be deduced from the masculine husks, tempted minds flittering over possible identities and the regularly shared details of each couple's intimacy. They shared all the weeping gore and empty conquest; the girls did the same. It was a matter of course to know how intimate everyone was, a matter of pride. Friends are great at depreciation. The gold-chained boy and the one with the sash shared more secretive glances. They each knew by sweaty experience what they should have known only by lurid story. Searching for the girls, they searched the suspicion in their friendship. They compared themselves; venom in their hearts to match the shadowy speculation in their brains.

On the field, runners slipped and fell, passes sailed wide. But the crowd loved the pile-ups of dainty wriggling bodies. Possession changed sides several times, but the game remained scoreless.

"What kind of game are you supposed to have with five-minute quarters?" the gold-chained boy said from within the shadow of the concession stand.

"They're girls, man. They get girl quarters."

"It's flag. What would you want out there anyway—bunch of ugly bruisers? Is that how you like em?"

Their wry laughter belched stale in the hot afternoon. Even in the shade they were sweating beneath the coarse wool. The second quarter approached, and it was time to finish their costumes.

"You wanna get ready," said the virgin, and he

gestured to the gym bag that concealed the flask. The others advanced toward the bag in assent. Sudden movement stirred their surprised heads dizzy in the heat.

Don't leave me, mommy. Mommy, don't leave. I want one more kiss. I know I said I didn't like when you kissed me in front of other kids, but I don't care anymore. Mommy, I'm afraid. Who will take care of me when I'm hungry. What if I'm hurt. Please. Please. Please. Please.

Tugging at a limp arm.

"Hey. Are you ready."

The virgin smacked the prodding hand away with a look of disgust. "Don't touch me."

"He's drunk," jingled the gold chain, dismissing the outburst.

The virgin dreamed of sucking on the flask like a baby bottle.

"Relax, it's right here." Up came the red sash from the secrets of the bag and produced a pouch of old make-up. Two lipsticks, a compact of blush, mascara, and a few tubes of eyeliner. All of it dried and untouched since it was last handled by the virgin's mother.

"Does your dad know you took this stuff," asked the sashed boy.

"No, he doesn't care." But that morning he had shut the drawer containing his deceased mother's last belongings so quietly while his stern father over-buttered toast in their kitchen.

The gold-chained boy uncapped the lipstick and began to smear it recklessly all over his mouth without hesitation, against its will, shattering its prudence. The virgin tasted the sting of his betrayal creeping up the back of his throat. The lipstick had been waiting so long for the return of lips that kissed so sweetly— at night when her child was asleep—and spoke so soft and gently. The gold-chained boy strangled the lipstick in his clenched fist and reapplied a wide swath of grotesque red over the skin surrounding his mouth. His laugh wild, exhilarated by the dress-up like the fear of being caught. A few brazen inches from the faces of the other two in turn, with his ridiculous mouth, his red laugh, whisky young and putrid on his breath. "Well, what are you waiting for?" he insisted.

The products lay strewn around between them like an expired expression of love, but more obstinate, like hospital instruments. The boy with the sash began globing dark circles of eye shadow above his eyes and covering his cheeks with large blotches of rouge. It was too dark, abusive and indelicate, he wasted its unwanting, forcing it. And it smelled like her.

You remained true to me because you died. Anytime life goes on there is betrayal. My footsteps who quieted. My wife in promiscuous windows. And I deserve it. I must be made to know myself. But I think of your caring smell of perfume and crayons and pies that meant I was safe. Then you learn: everything is false; everything is converse. There is no harbor.

The virgin quickly grabbed the remaining unopened lipstick. He held it in his hand like a wounded animal as the two others finished the first. It lay on the ground, its cap off, twisted all the way out, the base of the stick a crumbled, sloppy mush of red. The virgin carefully uncapped the one in his hand and twisted it up with gentle somber decision, raising it to his lips that had last tasted it upon hers. He kissed again—in his accismus. Kissed again his mother's lips. He angled it and tried to mimic the way she had applied it, slow and deliberate, not allowing any to run over his lips. He choked, slightly, but it was a fleeting sound, nothing more. He would not cry before the other boys.

You will learn to color within the lines—she promised me. Mercy, I forget where I came from. The supple love that made me real. That forgave me my wrongs—but my forgetting. Mercy, this is a new womb. I am sickly sliding over her beatitudes. Her memory makes me choke as on fluid. My lungs must come clear so I may breathe. Pouring in, pouring out, full, empty. Elynia, Elynia, quickening.

He slid the lipstick snugly into his uniform, careful not to lose it. The three boys stood together and strolled to the sideline, ready to take the field. A light breeze persuaded their skirts and wound round their thighs in a way discomforting and unusual to them, and they felt vulnerable to its intrusion. The alcohol enthralled their blood, played with their symbiotic excitement. They sweated more, impatient in the full sun, sweltering beneath the wool. The girls called a timeout to save a final play before the expiration of the clock.

The makeup twitched and spread with the film of sweat forming on the boys' skin, and it began to run down their faces in expectant beads and fathering dark portends. Black, blue, and red streaks sharply contrasted pale skin, leering grins, coy laughs. The cavorting boys flashed their ghastly faces of overdone tragedy towards the crowd. The streaks like veils, like jail bars; the captives peering through, begging the veil be lifted, looking like painful hymens.

The assistant principle counted down the final seconds, and the girls returned to the line of scrimmage. A few curious spectators in the bleachers gawked over at the boys' grotesque faces all waiting in a row at a distance. Friends elbowed friends, and the three created a little stir. The astonished crowd thought the boys were crying in humiliation, caught in girls' cheer uniforms.

Capricious blue eyes, my mother thought when I was born. She cried when she told me the story. I think she knew she wouldn't live to see me grow. Then she losing sight of her newborn's face to antidotes stooping blurry-eyed, turning her insides. Unconscious. She was awake, she told me, when they cut her. Then, I held her thin hand in my small fingers, as she lay in her non-verbal bed. And someone said I had her glazed eyes.

Halftime.

The storm moans without meaning. Contorts with no expression. Will not say if it is upset. It bursts self-extinguishing surrender, slathering an ungrateful lover, but intimacy is absent. The volume of rain conceals all emotion. At once indistinguishable fury and peace, billowing heights might sigh for sadness or leap for joy.

Some huddle dismayed beneath light-hearted awnings to wait out the storm, while a young man and woman are ending a conversation on the nearby sidewalk. Punctuated by the passion of the torrent— the rain rolls over their lips, dribbling like their inaudible words. He briskly turns away holding his coat closed against the rain. She watches, emotion indiscernible in her slightly open mouth. Onlookers ask one another if she loves or hates him too much. Head soaked, drops tenderly stroke the softness of her cheeks. No one under the awnings can tell if she cries. The storm hides her, secretive, mingling rain and tears, purity with salt, kissing the trouble from her cheeks and trembling lips. She shivers as they are kissed away.

The adolescent world waits to be informed, but the storm chatters on with the sidewalk where their conversation ended. The runoff carries away a thousand lucid tongues speaking nonsense, protecting emotion the storm stripped and slid into the gutter.

Another life I was acquainted with grandeur . . .

The man used to be pretty. Looked like young girls gave him trinkets of their affection. Though not yet old, he had the particular age that comes from getting everything except what he wanted. Now with coarse wavy hair retreating, skin turning dry, muscles turning flaccid, he wanted to buy a house for his compassion. To settle down, perhaps, to love someone still unknown. To make amends. But this languid compassion had just sparked to life, and quickly outgrew itself with earnest hope, courting a newness like an irretrievable past, slender and handsome, diminutive and inchoate. The search for a house continued for many months. A particular man through the pain of indifference, he considered every nuance of the contending homes. He did not want to work to repair them. New life should be immediate. The house had to be ready to move in, or as close as possible. Closing in on a final choice, the buyer labored over his investment, strolling indecisively once again through the empty rooms of his favorite, a brick house with roses.

I would slumber snuggled in the crook of eye-ascending architecture, but I have not slept. I cannot find the smoothly worn crook that my fetal body warmed and softened to slide along my length as soft as milk. Delectable, the lush and pulpy mortar; adding weight to bear weight. Was it another life I built palaces, a fool treading beauty.

The realtor, a bank representative, and the buyer had met at the house early in the morning, hoping to sign the papers at last. It was a two-story red-brick home, on an old red-bricked and tree-lined street, with a large front porch slathered in the sweet roses. It belonged to a grandmother who recently died. Her grandson and niece had prepared the house for sale. The niece left behind a bough of fresh wildflowers from her farm to brighten the kitchen for the occasion, but she was always gone before the buyer arrived. In the little kitchen, he was still pacing. He clasped his hands tight behind his back and swung each foot pensively to the side, then forward in a semi-circle, not bending his knees. Posture was how he affected control. He had a habit of letting each foot hover a moment while thinking, before grounding it, heel first, and then lurching forward with his weight. The realtor, sitting at the table, watched from the corner of her eye, crawling with annoyance, fixated until she heard his stalled and finely-polished shoe finally contact the floor.

The buyer's face carried a grave look of concern as his footfalls eclipsed the sighs of the realtor, who had come to despise spending so much time on what seemed a very unlikely sale. He searched for perfection in every nook and cleft of the house, every joint and joist from the basement to the roof. He swept back his sport jacket to seize a tape measure from his back pocket. In the same motion, he lowered to one knee and thrust his face near the wall. The realtor had watched this a hundred times. He passed his fingertips through his curly sandy hair, examining with strange attraction another specific detail of the house, the plaster work along a length of wall. Then on to review with delicacy the few troubling cracks, the shadows in each corner, the insulation, masonry, floors, and paint. The house brooded feral, waiting for him to decide. The seller and bank agent conspicuously checked their watches.

The buyer's sternness was contrary to his loving intent. Just as the sport jacket, well-tailored, concealed a landscape of atrophy. But it was the hope that the house would be a joyful place that made him determined that it should be perfect. At last satisfied, he reservedly made the decision that the house would be his.

Firmly braced over the kitchen countertop, he pressed a turgid palm beneath his square shoulders, the other coddling a pen like an artist, remembering. His hands were powerful, but gentle, their skin calloused and scarred, but clean, as though his hands had worked, had been tested, but not anymore. A brocade signature graced the papers; a great sense of pride swept over the buyer. The bank representative was shocked and relieved; he never believed the sale would happen. The realtor knew she would go for a drink. Standing on the porch as they locked the door, the man admired the frame of his house and thought he heard the timbre of its old voice, resonant within solid wooden ribs. He could sense the grandmother's patient, widowed hands that pointed the brick with muriatic acid, a supreme limberness in the scent from the roses climbing the lattice at both ends of the porch. The bricks were clean and the mortar crisp. They all left the house pleased with themselves. But the man had managed to pay far too much, because compassion, while insistent, was a bad negotiator.

A softened crook, wearing in the hollow where I wear out. To slide along a nameless faceless length and lap its milk, soft with groggy heat. I construct my own lonely confession, a monument to hearts like wildflowers, through which words would pass as unheeded sashes of wind between the playing fingers of color. I build—I articulate. I articulate as I beg. Where is a bed a bed a bed for worn out flesh.

The day after the sale, the new owner awoke early to begin his work on the house. He loaded tools and paint, and other supplies into his truck along with some necessities and a change of clothes. A little patching, a little painting, a few screws—he figured he could start to move the furniture by tomorrow. Meanwhile these few things would sustain him, and he could stay his first night in the house while he worked. He was especially excited to hang his photographs, which he had indefatigably collected since losing his affinity for paintings. He loved seductive silhouettes of black and white, both brash and subtle in long shadow. No color. Rayographs, limber forms extending negatives like tenacious maidens. To blush before the filament. Distilled curves that dissemble the body so a stomach is a sun-rising ocean or an instrument of flesh. Photos were truth. And even if the truth is hidden, once found it gives itself up permanently, without reservation. Unlike paintings that were unrequited images, not realties, that took all and gave nothing, and offered no discovery, only toil. The gifts of his own former paintings were only hypnotic emblems. He had been unable to gift the difficulty of their creation.

He arrived with the boxes while the sky was still a swirl of colors. His key raked bronchially against the tumblers of the front-door lock. But when he entered, his eyes began to burn slightly from the stale and musty air, offended by the sting of a solvent bottled in the house. He left the door open, for a fresh breeze, and assembled boxes into a nuclei, to work around them in the cell of his improvement. Already growing proud of his progress, he entered the kitchen with screws and brackets for the cabinetry. But a six-legged inconsistency caught his eye as it emerged beneath the stove, meandered a moment, lingering along the protective edge of the oven door, flaunting its antennae. It scampered to the far wall, and wedged itself into a crack in the quarter-round.

He grunted aloud, an astonished rumble rising from his gut. "No bugs were here before," he said, soured. The empty house swallowed his words the way a sad person might accept a debilitated confession. From his hands and knees, he peered into the trench where the creature escaped, fingered the ragged edge of plaster. "I thought for sure, these were sealed tight all the way around. Must've made a mistake." His surprise had him speaking to no one. He poked and prodded at the crevice and finally satisfied himself that he could do no better than to patch it; anything trapped inside would starve and be done with.

Would I have heaped myself upon a starving mistake. Thrust into a tangle of limbs: alive like fire until they are stoic like brick. Abandon myself for the tranquil surrender of confusion. Open my infestation. Shall I, sweet malady. Heap thick waiting within the succor. Resolve, in the leach of self gestating, princely to grievous craving. My other self drops to blackness, nourished by labor. I was slender. Then I was wanted, cherished. Now I am wanting, and mistaken with drastic clarity.

Bewildered, he stood and turned a more critical eye on his surroundings with the suspicion of instinct. All at once, elements of the house appeared different than when he bought it yesterday. The walls in the dining room were smudged and blackened. He had not expected to paint that room, but it direly required it. Next he noticed the pine floors in the hall and living room had nicks and gashes in the wood. He stooped over them to see if the cuts were fresh, but they were not. "How could I have missed these," he asked himself, rubbing his fingers over the pleasing tickle of smooth and shallow grooves. The pert wildflower bouquet on the kitchen table was already wilted like a stale, jilted love.

In the basement he found water damage for which he insistently searched before buying the house. The bricks of the east wall had gorged on moisture over the years. They were porous and puffed up; one touch would cause them to crumble, gnawing an empty hollow gaping in the side of the wall. The spongy bricks were not supporting the weight anyway, even if their regimented blank faces appeared to bear up the squeezing imposition of the impending house. The boards and beams, walls and wooden ribs supposed too much. Supposed themselves right out of existence, into a purgatory of the owner's articulation. The house flickered and hummed his warming clarity while silence burrowed into the owner like an unspoken indictment. Murmurs felt luscious, two-fold double-speak. Dripping down each inch into the cellar door. The hardwood floor rose gregariously to trip him where the edge of a board had warped, and he fell hard enough to split the edge.

Wood splinters at once, after drying and dying. Cracks one long peel, one long drag. The point scurries electric, wedging between sinew. This wood has been preparing a long time. And I die: dry and unprepared, bared to the rending invective that rockets through my shell supine as a board. Like that house I fixed, destroyed again by inevitable time. Dust invading the room where I lay isolated, a long jaw open-mouthed on the glimmering floor. Was it another life I built palaces. Another life I

David Michael Belczyk

was acquainted with grandeur. I am fast becoming shambles.

The crinkled eyes of the window sashes smiled at his humiliation. The windows dated from the home's original construction, including the large living room window through which one could so easily presume to see. They feinted solid enough to keep out the storm and constrain trespassers within their searching eyes, but in the century since construction they had slowly changed. Each pane had flowed down slow with time, thicker at the bottom than the top. With age the panes lost their sightlines. The imperceptible change apparent only at last to the lines of sight dissecting. Vision through the glass became distorted—bending light to dark, separation merged into contact.

I was exposed through the exposition, adoring, the pane of the window became my own. And I saw myself in your pain benediction. Before the window. You ancient bare note straining to hold. Hum. Dig you up in my panoply, disappoint myself with you, put you back. A note, singing to me again. Your steam, body, fluttering cut smooth in profile, wearing into my shielded crook. I note, the endurant maybe in the figure I knew.

Heard you were back—she said. That she was married. Going home to make dinner for her husband. And I watched her soft strong form in the glistening window light. But I did not kiss her. And she was gone. And her husband, the poor boy keeping his lipstick, got all my afterwards: his wife's

184

servility, my flowered innocence that fled him. But it was a little girl watching the rain who quenched my fire with denial, to teach me the path of the storm.

As he trespassed in each room, disappointment grew. The whole scene spun around him as he searched, sweeping aside a heavy fear of discovery. Behind the house the blue steel of train rails, spiked through gnarled wood into cold dirt, began to tremble. Puckered preparing to wail. The single track threw sparks overcome by a passing train. The tracks cried then roared, then cried again unsure if they felt sadness or anger. Sad because they lashed out; angry because they deigned to cry. All the while the owner had investigated the house he had seen the tracks but never heard the train.

Elynia, this is not what I created, only what I attained. Something possessed but not owned. Unfortunate like a prize gained through inheritance. Temporary intemperance of purchased luster. A dream of worthiness. Where compassion blinks and I tremble with fear and perplexity upon my brow. Sweltering in the leach of my dissatisfaction.

The owner resolved upon his work as light bent through the gullet of his antique window and focused to burn. More paint, sandpaper, spackle, wood, mortar, nails, and tools. The new pine boards smelled sweetly of sap. It was fresh wood, young like he was again, young to renew the old. The house was again hungry, growling, and empty. Nothing of time's anarchy could remain nothing.

I conscript pride to blush at my choice, but to repair that choice I ask nothing. Pride and desire are ornaments; I do not suffer their benediction. My skin is slight and wrists slender and they must suffer my patience instead. And the house told me—stop that abysmal preening.

The owner poured himself into the destitute home: tearing up the rickety, pitted floorboards to make way for fresh wood, sanding the grime and imperfections. Arms locked as back arched as he thrust the block of wood wrapped in sandpaper back and forth along the length of the floorboards. The owner cut and measured, dripping sweat making imperfect dark circles on the lighter wood as he crawled about the rooms. Working mostly on hands and knees, the skin on his hands wore dry and cracked until it bled. He sanded off the spots of blood that absorbed into the wood. The owner scrubbed and scraped the scarred walls. Patched their plaintive cracks. He mixed the absolving paint well so it would not run. There was no circulation in the air and his sweat came ceaselessly. He curled embryonically inside his labor, quivering within the darkening misshapen circles on the wood floor.

Fantastic chrysalis. Wrap me like a resurrecting pain. And I androgynous larva wriggling: what will I be.

He worked along the grain of the wood, clambering over the holes where he had ripped up the boards. He had creases in his chafed knees from the cracks and imperfections in the floor. Clean smells bullied out the stale air. Whitewash brightened new mahogany stain. Cleaned windows told the truth. Everywhere the house teemed with the cells it sloughed off. It did not resist but for the necessary resistance to help in its liberation. Profuse dust coagulated the putrid air. And the owner did a butcher's work, needing to clot the spill, to wash his hands, to keep the taste from his mouth. Open all the windows and let it run, run, run out. Why his face is contorting the past. Open the window. Close it again before the paint clogging on the track causes it to stick, like the owner's still-tacky mind flush with want. He stumbled up from his knees pale with effort and dizzy, wanting the night air of the open window.

Serene air, turned chilled, slid in as he stood, knees aching. Tomorrow, then tomorrow, then tomorrow; he taunted himself with the minutiae of his task. Starting from the dreamy caverns of toil that echoed in his mind's eye, the owner discovered himself, tactile flesh, blinking from the lighted glass with blackness beyond. An unfamiliar chiseled face looked back at him, rough with scruff and dirt. From his extended arms flowed hot and sticky absolution, its stench the fragrance of labor smelling worse with devotion. A potent animal leapt inside him hungry for what the house cured, an animal that prowled when he was strong and thin. And he put it down, begging sleep, fetal on the bare wood. He spent night after night alone in the house, asleep on the dirty floor from exhaustion, the wood dust caked in his inflamed nose.

Dig into the animal belly, spur it on, and it writhes to get free, lurching forward. Drive it further, drive it hard until it collapses from exhaustion and at last dies. From the top of this heaving hulk, enthroned upon a carcass, stop to see almighty beauty annexed, persevering trodden upon, and reach, reach from the husk. No longer wriggling. Now the same breezes sip from under the same windows swallowing sober awe—pregnant similarities envisage smiling, carrying unconceivable surpassing. I come out of a lifetime of slumber, cannot distinguish the haze of the moment from the haze of memory. Was it another life I built palaces. I am unnumbing through labor. The pricking needles of it slowly recede, and rejuvenated flesh lights up energized as an esplanade on parade.

I begin to sip at it now: something strange and unknown, created through the work and sweat of my shoulders. Attain the long dream, the cool, light samara, where silence twirls within speech of labor. Perfection infects then breeds, waiting to be accomplished, up out of my own fossil until the Pangaea becomes a mask cavernous, peeled its gluttony from my aged face and slid down over my chest ensanguined with toil. I may dwell in this palace, aching me hobbling arrogant mud upon coy boots to dirty the halls. The cold dirt loves what others have failed. Until the sting of my closely shaved face with pink parlor, blushing aperture, the pall of my expression. Make a god of the work and swoon.

For five months the owner worked alone. As the refurbished house emerged strong and unblemished, his shoulders grew into thick bulbous husks from the work, tight and flexing as he shifted. He had transformed. He was trimmed and tapered differently, pulverized within the pulp of a fleshy armor. His steps across the floors were light and punched with power not weight. Circulating room to room, he practiced the twist and bend of his new body, striding a new humility through his achievements instead of pride. He did not feel fault for choosing a house that required so much effort, but he speculated he had been distracted by a distortion of details. But now the house was nearly accomplished. Compassion was satisfied.

That night the owner took some fresh air on the porch. He snatched a broom on his way out and began sweeping the few squat steps that led to the yard. Their flat gray cement danced silver in the moonlight. Lightning bugs flittered between his head and the porch ceiling, filtering through the dark musk. Their play brought forth from his mind's forgotten recesses the memories of when he played as a child. There loomed the specter of childhood dreams—the shell of an abandoned building, rearing out of a spotless field. In the noon-light, it was a great theater, a pillaged city of converts, a pirates' lair, half the bricks crumbling to expose the insides. Scale the wall. He yelled when he vaulted over the porch toward patient hands. Into the house. And now he reflected that his house should be razed upon his death.

While the owner worked the broom briskly, he accidentally swept across a single bug that had lighted on the step, and scored it against the rough concrete, killing it. The torn body spilled its luster, glowed very bright aside his steps in the dirt. More bright but less alive. A brilliant alone with no dynamic, no volition, burning out the last of its illumination. It faded to a pale green, and before he stepped back inside, he looked and the light was gone.

At last the owner was down the larynx of the stairs into the catacomb of the basement, at the end of his task, scrubbing the sludge and muck from the floor after patching the crumbling foundation. There was a sudden spark of joy amid his work. Discovering himself in his new home that had labored away its imperfections and given birth to his new body. Even the shadows of the basement could not dampen the thrilling rush of recreation once the owner realized his achievement. In the dank and billowing dust from the waste he removed, in the cold dark of the cellar, where the rebuilding work concluded, the owner began to sing. The echo cracked slightly as it rose from his belly, resonating through the hard brick and up the stairs to the warmer wood where it opened full. The song ruminated deep in his lungs, spread from his mouth swarming beauty, sheaves of unfurling light that filled the house so it might burst. The tone undulated strong then weak, cringing to fade then lifting the boom of the rattling voice, lifted from within until he nearly choked on its immensity. The voice magnified his body amplifying inside the bellows of the house, tearing loose the last old coagulation. The voice wielded the owner's will through his ramshackle joints: titillated the bones scintillating up and down the scales, as he plunged the washrag into the water and brought it sopping back down to the floor. The thick rag slopped up the dirt. Plunge it again in the muck of the bucket. Little cuts on his knees stung where the soapy water crept into his cuts, pushing the wail of song to its brink.

He scrubbed on, crawling within the ancient remnant from which he uplifted his voice. Outside, a strong wind curled through the chimney in eddies that sent their howls through the hollow shaft to join him.

The work of creation, Elynia, is never finished. Until the final crushing gasp, I will create. Even in this tomb, I will recreate. It is my task to survive with the tools I am given. I can only surrender what I am. I exist to create my one visage. To make good from the waste; to believe from faithless matter. To make even the suffering of anonymity blossom. I almost choked to death at the age of two: built up like a rearing animal: now you see what issues from this frail figure!

Amid the storm, one cloud suffers a celebrated transformation. It began new and white, like cotton waiting to be stretched into thread, floating below its darkened siblings. But in the fierce rain from above the cloud is pierced, scourged and battered. Never is it stretched to a shape that can suture indefinite wounds. Instead, it weathers purity. Grows heavy, gathers in what towering clouds shed and then thickens to grey with their anger. Accepts the thrust of obedience. Becomes hard muscle, rigidly defined. And when it, too, pours out upon the ground it sheds the water that was its creation. The prism from the darkening cruet. Pours clear, then disappears.

Thought it might have been a way that God wanted to be close to me . . .

The waitress looked full of intent, as her firm but tender body flexed around tables, winding through the sinews of the restaurant. Black silk of her chin-length, strait hair pulled into a tiny ponytail, unveiling a mischievous smile on her kind face. The round hips of her petite body swayed side to side, brushing past intervening chairs and tired patrons that sauntered out of the middling restaurant past its dark wood paneling. They left tables piled with greasy leavings, sour vinaigrettes, desiccating salt, and florid lip marks on sweating water glasses. The waitress approached a cramped corner booth brimming with slightly-younger, blond charisma sitting upright against the wood-backed seat. It was difficult to sit comfortably as he watched her, and he alternated between a staumrel slouch and poorly-feigned posture. He had chosen the third of five booths along the back wall, a table he had spent years swabbing with dirty water, acting the role of obedient busboy.

At one time he knew the tempting woman impending now, but after more than two years since he left the restaurant, she mostly seemed a strange mingling of a waitress serving coffee, a trip to an old amusement park, and a brief spat with tuberculosis. Behind the waitress, the young man could see the bald owner peering his shinning glasses around the corner of the office door, ogling her as well. Even while already preparing to dock her the time she spent in conversation.

The waitress placed two full cups gently on the table.

Fresh hot dishes scald me like burning skin. The dishwasher pours swirling steam and its boiling discharge flows wasted into the sink. The drain is stopped with food, can consume no more. The water is rising. In the basin floats a soup of devoted half-eaten morsels: a quartered potato, slivers of string beans and carrots, vegetable skins and the waterlogged trim of a shredded pork chop. Small coin-like slivers purchase their way from mouth to plate to drain and down into the unknown. A valueless hot absolution of once-edibles.

He remembered the taste of her mouth.

"Really, I only need one," he said, smiling at the two cups full of light-brown; looked like the owner was reusing brewed grounds again. "It's not that late." His bleak voice wandered up a dissonant melody.

"One's for you, and one's for me. And, you know, you could have avoided this conversation if only you had come and gone before we slowed down for the night. You saw how many tables I had." She sat cautiously but made herself comfortable, planting her elbows and starring across to him.

"Thank you," he said.

"So serious!" She mocked his exasperated smile, pouting out the prurient lips of her small mouth. He gave her a quick up and down. She looked like a wine rack depleted of bottles. His mind exacerbated her judgment, whipping her words up like rising clouds into something worth careful consideration. He hated to be called serious, she knew that. He preferred the thought of someone pensive, attracted to pensiveness, becoming the attraction. The sorry folds of her face were much deeper than he remembered. He assured himself that he had not returned to see her anyway. He returned for selfish reasons: to see what he had left behind. But he lingered. She plaited her nonplussed fingers over his surrounding the cup and pitied him anyway. He must be lonely or he would not have come back. He was only ever good for accepting and not worth a second attempt at anything else.

It was so long ago that I knew him, when he was nothing but a little boy. You have to forgive me. You have to repair me, to piece my broken shards or I will cut. We had delicate wine glasses at the restaurant that came out of the dishwasher so hot, they would explode if you touched them. That was how he touched me. Like glass found in your food. New love animates the danger of the past less magnificent. Shards like crystals swirling in the gorged drain. Exsanguinating.

"What are you looking at?" he asked with flat expectation.

"I'm trying to read the look on your face."

"I'm just taking you in."

"Haven't you taken enough," she smiled. Then fixed him "Well, I'm taking in you taking me in." Lights extinguished throughout the closing restaurant, enshrouding their privacy. But the owner made sure to bustle through and annihilate it.

Strident across their takings, he asked, "How's life."

"You know how it is," she said. "Same as always, getting by with things the way they are."

"Only two people bussing now," he indicated two jovial boys at a bus station behind a half-wall of wood paneling, plunging an endless flow of dirty glasses into scalding water, down over a whirring mechanical brush. Hands and forearms scalded pinkish from refusing to wear protective gloves. Fingernails chalky, blood vessels contrasted vehement against scaling skin. The boys thought themselves concealed. One labored over the steaming sink when he noticed the other in the reflection of a stainless-steel dish rack above, creeping stealthily, silently winding a wetted dishcloth. The boy at the sink continued plunging the glasses while his eyes captured a second damp towel hung from the top rung of the dish rack. In a thin moment, he snatched the towel, spun, and landed a wet crack across the chest of his assailant. The bartender laughed over his shoulder as the busboy winced and lifted his shirt, revealing an emphatically raised red gash across his heart. Blood welled liberated to the surface. Waitresses doted the injured boy, rubbing his chest and cooing over him, chiding the other. Both wilted in the attention.

"I told the owner we waitresses are too busy for two busboys," she said. "We don't have time to clean tables. But, he says business has gone down lately and they need to cut back."

I love you, you little whore—he told me.

I love you, my precious one. But your empty tables are not my tables, without settings or even cloth. It is not my bare wood supine, courting the ceiling. Your empty chairs are not at my tables. Patient for some hope of hunger or service. Your plates and grinning forks are your own catastrophe.

You forsake your own heart's elect. I have the cloth, the glasses, and the pieces of silver to dress the table, but you have provided me nothing to serve.

I open my body before you to feast upon my hunger.

"You want to put something in that?" she asked of his coffee.

"No, I like it black," he said, still contemplating the consummation of consumption.

"I'm sorry, I should have asked you before. I can't hardly think anymore at the end of a night in this place. It's all getting so old." She took in a deep breath, "I'm working doubles all the time, and I'm so hot from being back in the kitchen I don't think I can even drink this coffee right now."

"But you brought it over." He flexed his overbearing brow like he caught her.

"I know. I'm just going to sit here for a minute, if that's okay." She was short on breath just from speaking. They looked at each other. At last, he moved toward the hand she had rested on his, pressing it between his hands. In the back, the busboys mopped the floor in the kitchen and the line cooks washed down the stainless. He could see them working through the double-hinge that swung back and forth each time one of the waitresses charged through. The kitchen door flopped over, oscillating, amplitude decreasing. Until it stilled to its center, closed on equilibrium and obscured his vision. The scent of soap and bleach shriveled the air like the skin of his hands when he had worked there, like her greasy unwashed apron wrinkled by endless nights with few tips, shriveled like their exhausted exchanges across the table.

Next-door, a mini-golf and ice-cream stand looked over the large red-brick house that had transformed into the restaurant. The man noticed the teenage girls in bright uniforms collecting clubs and shutting off the windmill hazard on number eighteen as he came in. A quiet girl from high school worked there when he was bussing. He admired her; she was vibrant and undiscovered. One day he walked over for his usual visit on break, but she was not at work. The other girls told him had run away from home, down to Florida to live with a boyfriend, or so they had heard. Then everyone found out about her father, what she was running away from. Beauty, fleeing one abuse to surrender to another. The cute teenage girls—the only ones hired to work there—still made a ritual of whispering the story to the new ones when they were alone at closing time. The man remembered the runaway he really wanted as he looked at the waitress.

Meanwhile, the waitress knew more than she ever revealed. The employees never washed their hands. The line cooks painted their faces with condiments and let out war whoops as they chopped heads of lettuce. There was a time she found the dishwashers getting high in the employee bathroom in the basement. They stumbled up to the kitchen carrying mountains of cold-cuts and winking audaciously at her. She stayed late that night like many others—after everyone had left, she and the owner in his second-floor office, when he had more hair. The owner found out about the dishwashers anyway and fired them all, though she swore to them she didn't tell. Then the owner fired her, on the pretext that she was with the dishwashers but really because of the affair. Then the owner fired the manager, whom he thought a threat because of his better looks. The waitress was back working the restaurant again after a week, during which she entertained a return to school that died on the vine. Only the waitress knew.

Encountering the man across the table again, she thought of skin. Hers was like a latch on a window, thin, warm, and slowly shutting, a window that bars the outside. There is much within to be protected. At first the latch is hard to close: then the paint begins to scrape away; eventually the metal is scored and shines bright copper through the surrounding white.

She clenched her teeth, "I used to have a better job. I used to work at a gift shop selling greeting cards."

"Wasn't that boring?"

"Not really. Everyone was happy. They were all going to either birthdays or celebrations. Or buy sympathy cards for someone else's suffering. Plus I got a discount." She remembered counting her cash drawer, then watching her manager count the drawer, then counting her drawer again. She was always short. The manager entered it into his book, and a list of meager deductions would appear on her paycheck under the heading: *Miscalculations*.

"I guess it's hard to imagine where we're going to end up," she said. "I just hope it's not here."

He stayed silent while she came to terms with something grave and unknown. The voyeur within him harbored a desire, just below his consciousness, that she would need his help and be reduced to sharing all.

I swear, you are my fidelity unto death. Life has stolen everything from me but you. You consume with love my battered body. Where else can I go to feed the hunger of my love. Here: I am the table. I am the wood supine for you. Eat. You own me. Only don't leave me.

I met you looking hungry, plunging glasses into the scalding water when you had no help. Little lines of sweat on your beautiful face. Plunging clear spotless glasses into that boiling turbulent caldron of dirty water. As though that would clean them because it was both caustic and dirty. Plunge love. Spotless clarity into consumption. I saved you and what thanks have I got. Plunge the glass again over the whirring brush.

Her brow turned down, "I just. . . I never thought I would be doing this. When I was a kid I used to think I was pretty and smart and I could do anything." The expression that pinned up the uninspired parts of her face quickly fell. The man's eyes lightened. The waitress's distracted hand searched her lips like slender glass delicate and helpless against the tips of her fingers, moist breath languishing a furrowed palm. The man lapped up the rhythm of her astonishment, fixated alternately on her peaked brow and the slits of her red lips peering through the jail bars of her fingers. Watching her chest rise and fall.

Do you have a hope or a lust. Or are you a lifetime spent with your hand covering your mouth.

"Go downtown, you'll make better tips." As he spoke, she tried to drink the coffee, and he watched her squint and pucker from the taste. She put the cup down briskly, rapping it against the saucer.

"And I'll tell you something else," she continued breathlessly as though not hearing him. "When I was little, I guess until I was about eight, I had this little box. I kept it secret and called it my *wish box*. It was from a toy jewelry set with my name stenciled on top. I decorated it with lace and purple sequins. It hid on the top shelf in my closet, which I thought was undiscoverable as a child because I had to climb up on a chair to reach it. My mother probably knew about it the whole time, now that I think back on it."

She took a second. "Everything I ever wanted or wished I'd one day become I used to write down on a piece of paper that I'd fold up and put in the box. I actually used to say *abracadabra* as I put each one inside for the keeping." Her head shook as she allowed an airy chuckle. "I was so stupid. I'd seen them do it like that in cartoons. I was going to be a beautiful actress, an adventurer-senator, class president, you know, if everything in the box really took." She did not seem to be looking at anything but gazed blankly at the table. "Sounds foolish now, I know."

"Why not?" he said, as though the question asked itself.

"Well," she hesitated, "I found the box a few days ago. Monday, I found it. I read every piece of paper in there, and not a single one of my ridiculous wishes came true. The things I wanted to be, I mean. My mom did get me a lot of that stuff for Christmas," she added quickly, to be fair. "So, I glued the lid shut with everything inside and threw the thing away. I'm not the person who's inside that box."

The scrawling hand of her childhood had not known what it would look like, looking back. That it would be so mistrusted. It just helped itself unwearily to a malformed alphabet. But it was not the familiar little girl that appeared over the sharp rim of the box when light cracked around its circumference after years of motionless rest upon a shelf. A strange and pretty woman with bleary eyes did violence to the delicate folds of a child's hand. Twisted up the ignorant pieces of paper that waited on the missing girl.

Why are we so deprived; what more could be expected of us than to wish. Thrown without knowledge or consent into the darkness of a sealed and tiny box. But we cannot wish away the past. Each of its secrets unfolds our parade of objectification. Making feasts of self-promises, folded up, tucked away, scribbled, folded; creases remain. We greedily expose each. Sated by sadness, ogling the diminishing hope plain on the face of the simple script.

"I think my father found it in the trash. I never saw his face so sad." She took another weary breath. "But, I don't know. Maybe he didn't." Her trivial treatment of the final few words decimated her sadness with indifference, like she disowned herself. He leaned in close to her, bridging the cold gap across the table.

"I'll tell you a secret," he whispered, "something I've never told anybody. When I was young, I used to have pain in my hands and feet, and along my side, where you can feel your heart. I liked to imagine they were the pains Christ supposedly felt on the Cross. Thought it might have been a way that God wanted to be close to me. But, one day the pains stopped. Once they went away, I felt abandoned, and

I didn't have those ideas any more. Which is a good thing because, like everyone else, I would have no idea how to be a saint."

She smiled while her fingertips traced the niche in his palm. "When did they stop?"

"Around the time I met you."

They laughed. And their still-born secrets died as they were first produced, filtered through the sieve of their disillusion without influence or consequence. He did not know if he should ever sweat dirty over the forge of faith. He did not know if: his platinum love hidden away from staining fangs. From humor. And though he did not show it, he had stumbled into a raw opened wound of youth, flooded with the sadness of lost simplicity. He remembered chasing lightning bugs over the hill in his back yard.

"I've got to close out for the night," she said and paused in a long look, "take care." She slid her hand away from his as she rose, leaving a patch of flesh over his knuckles that suddenly felt cold. Someone roared on a loud vacuum in the reception area as her back wound through the tables and dropped between the flapping kitchen door.

"You too," he answered in his own breath, an answer subsumed in the twilight of the restaurant. Nearly all the dining room lights were off now. The kitchen staff had vanished. He looked around the room. Then the coffee. He sipped from the cup, and it burned past his lips, scalded newly tender flesh vulnerable to its alkaline taste. He tasted every day since he had quit the restaurant, every day which she remained.

The owner still lurked in the small office by the bar. He sat at a cramped desk cluttered with five weeks worth of payroll, two telephones, and unused but threatening pink slips. His bald head and thick moustache capped by round glasses made him stocky and proud. The first in every morning—his face was folded with early mornings—he threw the doors wide with homage and fear, an owner's expectation that all within would be shambles, ransacked and looted by the robbers and beggars prowling the night. He dreamt uneasily about shattered china. He woke from his dreams of losing everything to returned each day, sweat upon his brow, turning his key slow, bowing humbly before the opened door.

Elynia, how could I confuse humility with servitude. O, Elynia, may justice be mercy.

Distancing clouds curl, spire, and flare, cantilever precariously over themselves. Mists bear down a ponderous, jagged edge tumbling full of supple white exhales. Each becoming a formless part of an infinite range, bearing its own inchoate edge, a different scale on an infinite range of scales. The cool breath of the clouds regroups on skin and resounds triumphantly intimate. Clandestine, clinging to secrets. The beads feel like a familiar identity, but rather they are the cloying of its absence. There is no protection; there is no other memory; and no sonorous incompletion.

ANOMALY IN THE DELICATELY FOLDED LANGUAGE OF THE RAIN . . .

A young girl, her face floating amid blond curls, pouted imaginary authority as she edged her saddle shoes toward the street curb. The afternoon had turned cold and damp with the storm. Rain licked the landscape a misty silver. The little girl isolated single drops at height and watched them gather upon the ground, bearing a horde of loosed flower petals beneath her protruding feet. A bright yellow mackintosh shimmered, unbuttoned down to her spindly knees, on towards where her eyes cast upon the coiling storm, overwrought by the serene and gentle touch of each drop, the power of small factions. Even as she should take refuge from their cooperation.

All forms of life bear similarity. Look alike, look alike! All forms of life! Swirling round and round a nuanced escape. Sickness in the pit of my stomach for any glory made through distinction. It rips through like infestation crippling a precious field. I cut out anomaly in the delicately folded language of the rain. To what end do I babble down the drain. What I have in common with all loss.

To keep her pretty dress and hair from getting wet, the girl eased back into the nearby bus shelter, eyebrows climbing high over round bright eyes at the wild downpour. The dirty shelter also teetered right upon the curb as though it were about to jump. The rain washed its filthy glass clean again. Rivulets like veins enclosed the walls of the shelter, and sealed its sultry womb within. The rush devoured her vision of the world looking out through the cracked and splattered window—christening illumination for the cathedral-like, somber dispatch. Imposing channels imprisoned the course of the rain over the sight-sealing carapace.

A raindrop pooled itself at the apex of the shelter's slanted roof. With the light push of a breeze, it clung on the cusp and began trickling down the wall, just inside where the shelter opened to the storm. It quickened inside and passed the face of the girl leaning along the wall, shielding herself in the sustaining apse. She noticed the little drop, followed it with her blue eyes. Her beaming face hovered near its meandering path. The drop felt her warm breath as it passed silently.

I am going now, down, as under an iron blanket, down through the teeth. And I am afraid. Please don't lose this place of my sacrifice. Oh, please, I am only memory. Don't diminish me so much as to forget the location of my sacrifice.

Somber smells permeated her awe, tickling her round, pink nose: swirling dirt, twigs, heaped dead leaves, paper and trash, bugs, spit, and sweat. Water wound down the worn pavement and exposed bricks of the street and charged the trough along the curb. It apprehended lingering litter, grappled it into the flow plunging towards a waiting storm drain. Longing and sorrow pawed ineffaceably from beyond the jail-bars of the metal grate that devoured the worm of the storm, ate its fill. The little girl obscured her vision of the metal teeth with white caricature apparitions of breath as the nearby drop reached the curb of the street below, unhappy to part from her. It had found its own steady path toward the open grate and could not break free.

Do not mock me. Grate defiler. Look from where I've come; do you see all that greatness above. I am part of that power, that fury. I must be strong. I must remember my origin and not depend on this meager earth; I will go back to the storm and return to my strength.

The little girl followed her drop, stepping back into the rain from the shelter. She stooped close as it rolled down the curb and towards the storm drain where water poured. Realizing the moment of loss, she stumbled upon a furious solemnity that is the fulcrum of the storm, presenting its myriad hands to succumb hearted capitulation. The earth swallowed the storm drop by drop, piece by piece unto entirety. Until the sky once again emerges blue, the earth will smitten for gluttony. The storm was beyond the guile of rusty teeth—teeth that did not dare the storm's majesty but rather wait and wait and smile always. The tiny drop, drawn unwillingly, winced to touch the cold metal.

I can create and hold this shape of a drop and be safe. Sphere like the earth. Collapsing toward my center conserving creative energy. I come free from the amorphous anonymity of the storm to be one. But don't I create this form to preserve it. Creation for preservation. Am I amorphous like my source—I am. I will self-consume to form.

The drop lulled along the stretching metal, tantalizing the teeth just beneath the worried face of the crouching little girl. It suffered now as it never did among the clouds. It did not revel in the thrill of its descent or rolling along its path. Instead it became aware of the gravity with which all other drops were pulled toward the grate, wondering at the inevitability of their flow. It was heavy now, burdened from its journey, filled with the dirt it had accumulated from those things left more pure by its passing. Robbed of its shimmer, the little drop felt itself pulled asunder from the storm. It searched wildly for new strength.

Shattered within your impenetrable being, Elynia; sift me through the sluice. Each string, tendril, strand—my lean meat hung upon your grate. You urge me let go. Let go. It is not by my strength that I remain. It is my lack of shape, weary without the spark of strength. Draped across the sharp edge, with a will I could not release. Without choice remain.

Still the girl stayed fixed, though the rain wetted her airy golden curls and made them heavy. Though the storm raged on, though infinite drops wended their way into the tomb of the earth, it was the one little drop that captured her devotion. It was small like her. And she also would not want to go into the blackness.

But the drop quivered with the torrent that preceded it into the unknown, as the grate sat stationed on its throne like remembrance only, crying hollow beneath the blue nothing sky. Gloating exuberant in exquisite parsimony. Unharmed in its indifferent weather: the storm invaded it or it invaded the sanctity of the storm. The grate swallowed everything flung down, without judgment and without disparity. Still the grate was unvoiced beyond its will. Stumbling from tacit, drunk strength into a pool of grief—it was force-fed succulent melody. Like living life atop a pillar only to be charged with vanity. Its solid metal bars could not stop the water from flowing. It would swallow the drop because it had to.

What strength is that to want: to be an unwilling glutton.

The girl extended a hesitant but curious hand, and the short-clipped nail at the end of her delicate finger nudged at the drop, thinking it might jump onto her like a lightening bug in her backyard. But the drop remained, precarious as ever. Her hand withdrew with something on it that came from the drop but was not the drop. She smelled her finger. Its soft pad glistened with a bit of ordinary water, but she looked at it like she did when she was cut, blood growing pregnant on her unblemished skin. She yelled into the storm drain—hello—maybe to find out where the drop would go, but she unearthed only an echo. Inclining her ear, she made out a plummeting sound then a splash of resonance like the rain drops were having a conversation.

She looked back to see the little drop had just released.

There was a sound of the unfailing sadness of hollow fixation. It fell silently, needing to persuade only a tiny column of air to pass through. And when the tiny sphere splashed at last into the great amalgam of itself flowing through the hewn underground caverns, it cried out mightily for the loss of its own shape. The cry played upon the mossy stone walls and down each corridor until it was merged with the cries of so many others, drowned out by the roar of their amalgamation. They were in the stream now, pouring out, and just kept falling.

The drop no longer knew itself but knew all from which it came. Not the path of the single drop, the storm in its completeness. Or even, the deceiving simplicity of what falls. The drop found itself in another, in another, until it found the power of the image from which it was made: the rush, the howl, the force, the current, that flows without the drops but sweeps them along in its power. And the little drop forgot to know itself.

Afterward, only a single certain shadow of blame: that the storm was over, is over, will be over. All its allies, aliases, everything reaped, all that traveled downward and fell together, even tiniest drops, had departed the dissonance of disunion.

It's nothing so unique that has cast me discretely over the boundary. Only the splendor of glistening streets and shimmering emerald leaves made me want to fall. It was the creation of the storm that had come before. And I thought perhaps this time I would not be left clinging to the rusted bars. I thought perhaps I could be part of the glory. Make no mistake—I do not venerate you but only your rust, which shows how you have swallowed me, time and time again. I don't want to pretend. I am so tiny and weak, I fly to your protection to shield me. Now may I go the way of my companions.

The people on the street find peace in the washing and wasting away. Their dirt carried down a hole in the earth and it disappears. Who could believe at the other end of the disappearing, beyond the pearly veil of folded pooled petals, a generative cocoon emerging. Great ferocity destroys the folded-petal orbs watching disappearance through the grate, but the water just carries, caries, turning the curve of the precipice with prophetic grace. Watch wide with the awe of adulteration: the great storm writhing and wrinkling in a rush from imperial heights, descending through the sluice. Trickling, gurgling with the grime of the street. Tearing down from the omnipotent sky its proclamation.

Trickle water drop. Trace. Loose, meandering track dirty from what you remove. Land in the lap of my silver lake. Turbulent, the tendons of my movements, guilty and praised. Trickle tender drop, mark of my mighty river—round running resistance, lingering, hanging, as I am prepared. Little drop. Release.

EPILOGUE

The young boy wrapped in his favorite blanket on the porch swing reveres his grandmother, who embraces him in the agile anticipation before the storm. The pleasant sun of the graveyard this afternoon has been eclipsed by the mounting clouds. Roses creep along the lattice, spilling their scent over the two, and the broad, old wood swing along the brick wall at the end of the porch creaks and pops with their gentle rocking. The rusty chain groans as they await the rain together. But the rain is patient; it can outwait them. On the sidewalk that borders the small front lawn, leaves swirl clockwise then drift away on eddies in the restless air. The boy watches them spin and hears their frail crackle scuttle on the ground where they laud in humble simplicity. Above the street of the small town, a foreboding sky darkens. Thick clouds have lost their texture to a mute, unbroken gray like static eternity.

"It'll storm any minute," his grandmother tells him. The boy cannot answer because his mouth is full of watermelon from an alabaster bowl by the swing. "Don't swallow those seeds," she hurries to add, "they'll grow in your stomach." He spits one over the side of the porch, causing his grandmother to roll her eyes in adoration of his honesty. The boy takes a big sniff. To him, the coming storm smells like wet pennies.

And the wind freshens. The leaves begin to circle faster. Elevate elated, turn silent in their rejection of the ground. They leap into a roiling barricade, and he is afraid they will whip into a tornado. Not knowing much about tornados, he figures they must start small and grow big, as with most things. Maybe they can grow quickly, he worries. His face transforms astonished as he sizes the slack offal of the eddy's central eye.

"Better go pick up the yard or the laundry will get wet." His calm grandmother rises and descends the porch stairs into the tiny lawn, near those spinning leaves, and heads for the clothesline in the backyard. But her gait is unsteady as she negotiates the slant of the lawn, and her frail hands swat at the air, clutching for balance. Her grandson, erect on the swing, sways with her nervously. Clothes are not worth the danger, he thinks. The wind might level her. Just before she is out of sight he yells, "Watch out for that tornado!" A man passing on the sidewalk glances up, perplexed. His snubbed face noses its way toward the boy, flat and unwelcome.

Elynia, a blood red ribbon cutting the landscape of my apotheosis. You are the first drops of rain to mark upon the bone-dry earth: the clod that is my mind's moist genesis of you, gushing as water from a rock, as from a victim. And ultimately it is cold in the rooms where people die, even when there are sweet roses in the sunny room. Roses we took from the lattice.

His grandmother pauses and lets her shoulders fall. He thinks she sighs, but when she turns slowly he sees she is smiling. She saunters to the porch to embrace him, "Oh, there's no tornado," she says, hushing him, hugging him tight. Then, the rain begins to gush, and the sweet-scented laundry flares, wicks the storm, and will have to be left to dry over again.

The boy looks down at the heavy, gnarled hand squeezing his shoulder. "Your hands are cut," he notices.

"From the roses I pruned."

The chill deepens and light diminishes. A blind *tap-tap-tap* lightens on the listless. Trees shiver, aroused by the exiting wind. There is an opening in the clouds like a door that has been cracked. Tentative fingertips push against it, in and feel it plying. Its emergence cuts a curt, scalding gasp, pastel setting nothing. Nothing set aside for season. Set upon a rocking blaze now gone, holding stillness, windless, clutching heat balled up under cover. The little center of heat who will not be there to see her loving eyes go facile underneath their blankets—refuses the silence coming from inside the sky down through the grip of hands pricked then clotted. Calloused with the devotion of work. Strength in the sustenance of sacrifice. His mind creates the sky like an open chamber of the heart preparing to drench the world or consume it in love and extinguish it.

"When the rain stops, I'll pick the ripe tomatoes from the back. It'll be too cold tonight, it stormed too long and it's too dark to pick the grapes. We can do it tomorrow. You can smash them with the two-by-four."

"Tell me a story until then."

His grandmother examined the stern sheets of rain. "I remember when my friend the shoe-man died. A local boy was getting married, and all the groomsmen gave the shoe-man their shoes to shine. Well, the morning of the wedding the groomsmen went to pick up the shoes, and the store was all locked up. None of them had money to buy new shoes, so they came right up this street here looking for shoes they could borrow."

"Who'd they borrow shoes from?" he asked his grandmother.

"They just went knocking on doors and asked. They asked me, but I didn't have any men's shoes to give them, you know. I saw them later, running back down the street as the church bells were ringing the hour. They were late. Some found black shoes to match their tuxedoes, but some had brown or burgundy shoes that didn't match at all. One boy was running along in plain white socks, all dirty from the street. They hurried up and waited, though, because the bride ended up being much later. Much, much later. So late that, after while, everyone had to leave."

He imagined a solitary figure wavering inchoate—the groom, the bride. He thought of the groomsmen in an empty fire hall gathered in a small group to fold wooden chairs and ruminate over failed vows.

"The groom-to-be was a musician who used to play at the local dances. They sure looked glum bringing back those shoes the next day. Everybody asked them, how was the wedding."

"And what did he do?"

"Well, what does anybody do. You go on, try and make your mark, though you don't know if you'll do it or how you'll succeed. Or even what that means. And eventually, you forget, or at least you won't think about it often. It'll be like that with us too, you know. I remember the shoe-man, but one day he'll be forgotten, too. You and I will be forgotten. Everything of this world passes away. And that's hard to know, when you're old like me. It's like being a bride, getting ready to walk down the aisle, and you love the groom so much it frightens you. But he waits there, faithfully, for everyone."

"I won't forget you," he says lovingly.

"Oh, I know you won't, sweetie," she says, her fervent voice with a husky crack. Then she kisses him, beaming with the warmth of joy. "And remember, little one, when the sun comes out in the storm, you get a rainbow, one of the most beautiful things in the world. And it lets you know the storm is over."

Sunset nears behind the curtains of rain, and the sky presses in a more forgetful gray. The storm is busy constructing the final details of its own demise. There is only so much rain, and it fears the inevitable last drop. It grows thin and fragile now, because of its fear, because of its ceaseless gifting, pouring out. The storm is confused by what is happening and shifts about, timid and pitiful. The sun appears just before it sets, past the storm's body on the fringes of horizon. Bursts of light clutch together on the ground, stretching out remnants of the daytime stolen by the storm. The fleeting glitter smears thin upon the ground.

"Will we have a rainbow now," asks the boy.

"It doesn't look like it, no. But you have to be patient."

The clouds forget their shape, forget their unflinching stature, and gird a crumbling primitive love out of trust in a cycle of being. They rose from the earth, leavened by the sun that shares their same demise, and now pour back into the mud from which they will come again. The storm rains until it is no more—pouring all of itself down upon kind withering embers. Crippled clouds falter and collapse to the earth, transfigure rain to a heavy mist and the storm breaks into white wraiths floating across the ragged lawn. The world becomes obscure as it finds itself again, invaded by the blinding white opaque in low rays. Tree tops shroud silhouettes from the diffuse milk sky, and the houses hide along the street, all directions discernable only for short distances.

The rusty chains of the swing moan plush garble prophesying the storm's death. The pallid storm, at last upon its back, gathers one final squalid blast to sail its dank wraiths through the paralyzed windows of the mind. The storm exhales and kicks grit into the pastel peace of ending, kicks grit into their memory.

Elynia, Gilgamesh, Valentine, strength perfected by the persistence of imperfect love. A lustrous first citizen of tragedy. You went before me. Like the storm we watched. I follow you into the night where memory dies. Boxed into the stasis of your meager possessions, lingering years after in my cold attic. I follow you into the neat garden rows you showed my ignorance. You teach me with pain, because, how beautiful the courageous heart that endures. But I miss you. Where are you.

The world turns upon the axis of their embrace, building up the momentum that makes the boy's insides twist. A chill resolves in the mist-grey gloaming, and his grandmother retrieves the blanket to cover the cold boy again. He is wrapped tight again on the front porch swing, and she sings nursery rhymes before the backdrop of the ceasing rain, singing in her native language that he does not understand. And even the fantastic and mysterious sounds the boy will one day forget, as she will forget even his name before she goes mimicking the storm. But now, even in the dead of winter, she keeps him warm enough to enjoy the swing for hours. The storm possesses only tumult; it cannot replicate the peace of her embrace.

Elynia, I am your precious one. In a haze emerged from sleep. Your skin like parchment, rough but delicate, smoothes my face. I read the lips of your continents; make you curious. Your wish pushes like a pin into. Me, Elynia, I am your precious only. Hold me tight as the descent of your image, wrapped a willing captive as you sing inscrutable, bringing joy, making white haze with your words that rise and walk.

Dark and wind at last coax the two inside the house. His stomach growls; he is hungry but wants to continue being embraced. Though she resolved to do other chores, his grandmother still wishes to embrace him. With his blanket about his shoulders, the child climbs upon her lap as she settles into the brown rocking chair. They rock a great unlamented arc across the sky. He closes his eyes, listens to her sigh, and smells her perfume. It hints at the sweetness of her roses that always cut her when she sought their beauty. But also the musk of the potato peels and eggshells that she threw on the garden, the soil mixed with sweat, toil that produced her fruit. But just a little, too, like holidays, when she did her hair in curlers and slid her huge car into the driveway full of spicy pies, and he would feel her soft patterned blouse, sitting next to her at the table.

"You are my *precious* one," she assures with an aged whisper.

He falls asleep, subsumed entirely into the rocking rhythm. Soon she fades with him, rocking away one memory at a time: the creaking front porch swing, even during winter, the chains rusting further with time that are sharp and pinch the hands; the shoe-man and his beautiful wife who had lost everything but their devotion; the husband she gave away to the maw of violence that drank his will; a faded picture she gave her grandson; even the brown cushioned rocking chair creaking to speak another year of age. As she rocks, the metal frame wears rough and scraps against the springs compressing like aged joints, voicing worn agony. But the boy has become immune to such a sound and sleeps undisturbed.

Elynia, in your sleep I build elusive oblivion. An origin unfit for knowledge. The unimaginable tower of human pity and its lookout is not high enough to see this origin. I will call it forth. I will ask it of you. Forgive my asking.

It is late. The laundry has dried again. He stirs to find he has been moved to the couch while asleep. One eye opens, and he sees his grandmother folding the laundry with the gentle touch of her hands, little mindful wrinkles of skin. She creases the fabric of a white sheet. A hollow catches shape and will not flatten. She eases it down, hushing it, assuaging frayed ends. Frayed trappings trap the loose ends of the boy's sleepy mind, bind like memories that will forsake him. His grandmother already soothes the memories, running her hands again and again over the clean warm white, soft submission working against her own pricked fingertips mending. He looks outside at the hazy black, the implacable stillness of aftermath. The stilled storm's ingrate emigration. She is startled by the muffled sound of his head against the pillow and embraces him a last time, while his eyes stay fixed on the bygone storm.

What I am for you terrifies me; what I am with you consoles me. We have misspoke and battered

*hope. Our tongues have slipped. But our bodies can
mouth our eternal pronunciation, if they can only
learn to open.*

Each of them is safe inside adoration. Safe inside
blanket and home and duty. Safe inside the prolonged
bite of their love from the storm of marching time
and its eternal human howl to which they would join
their voices. They shelter one another, while what
they have endured and what they will become rages
inevitably just beyond the walls of their embrace.

And then she smiles.

And then she smiled.

Elynia smiled. And they flow forth: foolish youth,
escapist girls chasing their own denials, little children
who miss their history, men full of bad loves and
seeking repentance, believers who martyr themselves
with the slit of their devotion, searching people who
would die for legitimacy, the toilsome with burdened
hearts, immigrants pouring into unfulfillable
dreams, emigrants plunging into the unknown like
rain, all those forgotten with their names washed
clean to ineffable monuments. The pyre of words
words words collecting their lives shed off from The
Ineffable. All of them looking over their shoulders
burning with the mystery from which they came.

Wake up, child. Wake up. Today corpuscles wrench
free by will from the immortal thirsty mouth. At
once the bold womb and the breathless wrinkle, at
once the mourning and the mourned. Bite that lip
and slit; issue as creation stings.

My love for you is above the highest risen clouds,

springing from deeper than the rain will sink.
Humbled by the soft squeaks of a rocking chair. Your
love leaves my troubles lost and tucks my youth
safely in its bed, wrapped in my blanket and nursery
rhymes sung in a language I can't speak. The joy of
the front porch swing in bitter cold. Wrapped in my
blanket, youth departing from me looks an awful lot
like love.

He hears even now in those mysterious lullabies:
"*This night will fleck off itself like obsidian. Honed*
to the spectacular shine of a razor's edge. And it
is so enthralling. We have pasts now, and we have
lost many things. But this night will end its fatal
separation, and we shall again reclaim you. You
will know my love again. The supreme purity of my
child's unabashed embrace. We will turn, turn the
soil of the garden again, turn it and purify it and
watch all those beautiful fruits grow. Wait, won't
you, for this advent. We will be together again."

God in the longing apparition of my child's
hands. In my innocence. In my precious thirst that
drowns. In the roses clinging to the porch lattice.
God in the slather of allegory—up and down with a
sharp reflection. God the knife's edge. God in aged
love that chides—don't eat those seeds, they'll start
growing in your belly. God in the slender coffin
of my throat. God that opens the words that pour
from my lips like a wound. In my own stranger
identity that I cannot touch. God in the eternity
of the unchangeable moment: create me becoming
everything. God that brings life to teach us to die.

God in our jaws like jaws, eyes like eyes, creating you innumerable. In the pain of love. In toil. God that washes our names to nothing and steals our testament. Transform this suffering! Let it enter like a seed piercing my anonymity, blossoming into a royal gift. So pretty is my ever-glory, ever-valiant; I am the armoire open to receive the sacrament. Here, here, use the good hangers.

9 780984 428823